The White Jacket

KATE NORWAY

The White Jacket

Originally published as Harlequin Romance #642

Harlequin Books

TORONTO • LONDON • NEW YORK • AMSTERDAM • SYDNEY • WINNIPEG

Original hardcover edition published by Mills & Boon Limited

ISBN 0-373-00642-X

Harlequin edition published February 1962
Reprinted 1962

This **Harlequin's Collection** edition printed 1976

A special note of interest to the reader

Harlequin Books were first published in 1949. The original book
was entitled *The Manatee* and identified as Book No. 1 — since
then some two thousand titles have been published.

As readers are introduced to Harlequin Romances, very often they
wish to obtain older titles. To supply this demand, Harlequin
prints an assortment of "old" titles every year. Some are made
available to all bookselling stores via special **Harlequin Jamboree**
displays. Others are appearing in the **Harlequin's Collection** series.

As these books are exact reprints of the original **Harlequin
Romances**, you may indeed find a few typographical errors, etc.,
because we apparently were not as careful in our younger days as
we are now. Nonetheless, we hope you enjoy this "old" reprint and
apologize for any errors you may find.

Printed in Canada

CHAPTER I

"RING, if you need me," Vivien told Nurse Wentworth. She looked back down Ward 9. "I've written up all the pre-meds for tomorrow, haven't I?"

"Yes, Miss Bromwich, you have. Mr. Malcolm will be doing the whole list himself, won't he? Because if the R.S.O.'s doing any of them I need to know, on account of the prep." She smiled faintly. "You know how he insists on mercurochrome."

Vivien nodded, and smiled back. "Yes, we all have our fads," she agreed. "No, the R.S.O. isn't planning to take any of them—not unless there's any last-minute hitch." She moved over to the double doors, and Nurse Wentworth darted to open them for her. "If that's all, then, I'll go and get some tea. If there's any left."

There probably wouldn't be, she reflected, and Winnie was always so difficult about making a fresh brew. She ought to know, by now, Vivien thought, that human beings don't tick like clocks.

She left her white jacket in the changing-room and put on the blue cardigan she had left in her locker before she went over to the Residents' House.

She had been right, there wasn't much tea left, but it was easier to make the best of it than to revive the perennial argument with the dining-room maid. She was alone, balancing her cup and saucer on the arm of her chair, when Johnny Dysart came in. He dropped a token kiss on the back of her neck as she skimmed through the evening paper, and amiably ruffled her hair.

She ran her fingers through it quickly, and looked up. "You're late."

"Um. Long queue for my boss's O.P. this afternoon." He felt the big teapot, and sighed. "You going to this hop tonight, Viv?"

"That tea's stone cold. Ring for some more—if you dare. Are *you*?"

"Depends." He lay back in the armchair beside the

fireplace and stretched his long legs. "Whither thou goest I will go, I expect. I was brought up to believe that betrothed couples were one flesh, socially speaking. Do we go, or don't we?"

Does he want to, or not? she wondered. It wasn't easy to tell with Johnny. His comfortable cheerfulness never varied very much. It had been his consistent good temper that had attracted her to him in the first place: it was the foil her own less equable nature needed, she knew. Johnny had the capacity to pluck her without effort from the depths of her occasional depressions—and to damp down her less reasonable enthusiasms with the dew of common sense. Big and confident, he made her feel safe.

"He'll be very good for you," her mother had said, when she talked about him at home. "You may be the bright one of the family, Vivien, but you're not as stable as a doctor ought to be."

She looked at him again, noticing how relaxed he was, lying back in the chair lazily considering his toes. "All right," she told him impulsively. "We'll go. But we may not be one flesh for very long—I'm on call."

The housemaid put her untidy head in then. "You ringing, Miss Bromwich?" she demanded. "Because it's Winnie's half-day, and——"

Johnny switched up his dipped smile to full beam. "Tea, Dorothy, please. There's a dear."

She stopped scowling and reluctantly picked up the pot. "Oh, it was you, was it, Doctor? Well, I'll see what I can do. But you'll be having your dinner——"

"Bless you." He closed the door behind her and went back to his chair. "Really, the eager way that girl springs to minister to us.... You want to go, then?"

"If you do, Johnny."

"Darling, don't let's have another of those 'which would *you* like?' sessions! I'm easy. Actually, I do feel it might be letting the side down a bit not to turn up because, let's face it, there are never enough males to go round. You don't mind if I put in a few duty dances?"

"Why should I? I suppose you mean with dear old Sister Blount? Not to mention that odd girl with the white eyelashes? That isn't what I'd call competition!"

The door bumped open again and they both watched Dorothy slap down the teapot and grudgingly gather some of the crumb-strewn plates on to her tray. When she had taken herself off Johnny said, "The odd girl with the white eyelashes, as you call her, is one of the best theatre staff nurses we've ever had in this benighted place. Not," he added, as he spooned sugar into his cup, "that it isn't an unnerving sight, those rabbit's eyes over a mask. But you can't have everything."

"Indeed you can't. And until our engagement's official I can't expect to monopolise you, can I?" She smiled. "It's not Staff Haggerty's white eyelashes I mind so much, really, as the fact that for all she knows you're still footloose and fancy free, and there for the winning."

Johnny put his cup down and sighed contentedly. "That's better. I can't think why I develop such a thirst in Out-patients. Well, that was your idea, my love. 'Let's keep it a secret for a little while,' you said. Admit it!" He came across to sit on the arm of her chair, and she thought again how safe it felt, leaning against his shoulder. "You want to announce it now?"

"No." She shook her head. "I know *me*, Johnny, and I want to feel a hundred per cent sure."

"Don't you, yet?"

"In a way. . . . I think I am. But if I'm going to let you down I'd rather do it before everyone else knows."

He bent his head to kiss her briefly. "You're not going to let me down, honey. If you do, I shall—I shall propose to Staff Haggerty!"

"Darling, no! She'd be sure to accept instantly. And she'd look even more like an albino rabbit across the breakfast table than she does over a mask." As she released herself and stood up little Bill Stedman trotted in, with his stethoscope dangling from the pocket of his jacket.

"Lord, what a day! Any tea left, Viv? *Who'd* look like an albino rabbit across the breakfast table? Not the new theatre sister, surely? She's an absolute bobbydazzler! She——"

Vivien left them to chatter and went up to her room. She wondered how Bill, who was Dr. Jameson's house physician, knew so much about fresh people on the surgical side. And she was surprised to hear that the new theatre sister had arrived already: Sister Blount had been on duty all day, and she had said no good-byes.

She fished in her wardrobe for a suitable dress. It wasn't done, or so Rena Todd had said, to make too much effort for these hospital do's. Rena had been at Queen's long enough to know, working her way up from dresser to registrar. "After all," she had remarked, "it's the nurses' hop. Leave the limelight to them. They resent us as men-substitutes, as it is, without our stealing their thunder. If they had their way all Residents would be strictly male."

Rena was always a little bitter on that topic. It was not surprising, after losing two bridegrooms-elect in succession to members of the nursing staff, Vivien thought. In Rena's shoes she might have felt the same. As it was, she felt a little sorry for the mass of the nurses, cooped up in their Home, lacking the easy camaraderie with the men that would have added healthy astringency to the atmosphere. They're right to feel we score over them, she thought. We do. Not in being blessed with unlimited opportunities for dalliance, which is how they see it—there's no time for that—but because we keep one another sane on the bad days.

The grey schappe silk would do, she decided. She held it up in front of her and considered herself in the long mirror. It did nothing for her pale skin, she knew that, but it toned with her eyes, and against her black gamine crop anything tended to look slightly gayer than it really was. Johnny liked it, she remembered. The first time he saw her in it he had said, "You look like a little Quaker girl in that, Viv, *au naturel.* But with a touch of rouge or something you'd be the complete vamp, I can't think why. Is that what the fashion writers call 'deceptive simplicity' by any chance?"

She said that she supposed it was, and that it had certainly been deceptively expensive for what it was, only Mother had insisted on buying it for her when she had first landed the house job.

Rena came out of the bathroom as she went in, with her metallic yellow hair hanging loose over her purple kimono. "You too?" she said. "I can't imagine why we bother. The dear nurses will *not* be pleased. But who cares?

8

I shall wear white chiffon, and silver eye-shadow and my most mysterious perfume, and play them at their own game."

"You know perfectly well you won't, Rena. And you must be far too tired to be the *femme fatale* after the list you got through this morning, and Mr. Drood's O.P.s since. I'm surprised you're thinking of going at all."

"My boss, bless his heart, thinks that an afternoon's O.P. is just what I need to set me up after lounging about in the theatre all morning. Golf! I hope he three-putted."

She looks worn out, Vivien thought. And how hard she sounds, these days. She isn't getting any younger—and it's beginning to show. "Why don't you make it an early night, Rena? You don't *have* to be eternally keeping your end up. Relax for once."

"It must be so nice to be able to," Rena said, with a tight little quirk of her lips that was meant to be a smile. "I'm not built that way, Vivien. If I'd been able to be cow-like, I wouldn't be where I am now."

And where is she? Vivien asked herself. She turned on the taps and opened the window to let out the heavy, cloying perfume of Rena's bath essence. She's got on: she's a registrar, and that's something. Half-way to being a consultant. But she must be years older than I am, and it's lonely at the top. Especially if you're a woman in a man's world. Thank God, I haven't her brains and energy —they must be a dreadful goad.

*　　　*　　　*

Johnny was waiting for her in the hall, sitting easily on the bottom step of the stairs, and they walked over together from the Residents' House to the gap in the main block, two hundred yards up the road, where the flagged path ran across the gardens to the Nurses' Home.

"A good thing they built this new Home," Johnny opined. "You weren't here last year, when they used to have all the hops in O.P.D. People sitting out in all the clinics, and casualties having to fight their way through the mob.... Doesn't *seem* a year since I quit the medical side."

It didn't do, she thought, to encourage Johnny to dwell

9

on his apostasy. He had been so sure that he wanted to be a physician....

"Don't tell me they managed to dance on that floor?" she said quickly. "It must have been murder."

"Well, hard on the feet, a bit. You look nice, Viv. Neat."

"You say that every time I wear this dress. That's why I nearly didn't."

"Don't you want to look neat, girl?"

"I sometimes think it would be a change to look a little gaudy. But Mother says I'm the boyish type. Only when I hear Rena Todd threatening to arrive in white chiffon and silver eye-shadow it does make me feel rather submerged."

"The devil she is! That *will* put the cat among the pigeons, and no mistake, won't it?"

"I don't think she really will. But I think she'd like to. Only she's too good a sport. Johnny, she looks so tired these days. What's wrong with her?"

"Always been the same." He threw one arm round her shoulders and steered her up the Home steps. "Too much ambition, if you ask me. Rena's determined to be a Great Surgeon—and if she only knew it she'd probably be a darn sight happier being the Little Woman to some nice chap."

"You think so?"

"Don't you?"

She shook her head. "Only half of her. The other half wouldn't be satisfied not to be up and doing—it would rust. She's not a cabbage like me. I don't want to be a career woman all my life."

"Then that's all that matters." In the soft light of the dance floor he smiled down at her. "I'd hate you to miss anything, Viv, through taking me on." He held out his arms. "Come on—let's dance."

On the second corner she said, "Johnny—Sister Blount's watching us with an eagle eye. You'd better have your duty romp next, hadn't you?"

"I will. Romp is the word: she only knows the Lancers, if you ask me. But she's a nice old duck. I shall miss her."

"Not when you see her replacement, you won't. Not if she's everything Bill makes out."

"I'm a one-woman man, remember? Not for me the delights of the chase. My hunting days are over."

"Are you sorry?"

He held her a little more tightly, and rested his chin on top of her head. "Terribly. Can't you see?"

"If you do that," she warned him, "there'll be no need for any announcement. Can't you manage to look just a little less enthusiastic?"

"Certainly, Miss Bromwich! I do beg your pardon. I can't think what came over me." He swung her round in a reverse turn, with her skirts flying. "You're sweet, Viv. When I get through with my duty romps, as you call them, I shall take you outside and——"

"Excuse me, Miss Bromwich..." Nurse Grover, from the theatre block, tapped Vivien's arm from the edge of the floor. "You are on call, aren't you?"

They stopped dancing and joined her. "Yes, Nurse. What is it—an emergency?"

The girl nodded, and a lock of curly brown hair flopped out of the front of her crisp cap. "Miss Todd has a strangulated hernia to do. She wondered if you'd assist. In twenty minutes—I've just switched on. Shall I say you're free?"

"Of course. I'll come straight up." She turned to Johnny. "Sorry, my dear. I did warn you."

"See that you come straight back. Meanwhile I'll go and make Sister Blount's evening for her—she likes to jog around with me. And I shall be quite safe with her, you may be sure." He squeezed her hand and released it quickly.

*   *   *

Rena was already scrubbing in the theatre annexe. She nodded to Vivien. "Sorry to muck up your evening. But that's how it is."

Vivien, hunting along the row for gumboots that wouldn't swamp her, shook her head. "I expected it, Rena. But why are you doing it? It isn't your firm's take in. Where's Mac?"

"Off to bed with one of his colds. So I stepped into the breach."

Vivien found the boots she wanted and kicked off her

shoes. If Sister Blount had been there she would have hurried guiltily to take them into the surgeons' room. "I see. Not satisfied with twelve hours' work, is that it?"

Rena elbowed her taps off and stood back to shake the droplets from her forearms before she went through to be gowned, and Vivien began to scrub her own hands. The antiseptic on the nailbrush made her skin tingle. Roddy MacBain off again, she thought, and the whole night to go. Did Rena imagine she could take all the night calls, as well as doing the lion's share of the day's work?

While she powdered her hands ready for the gloves the junior had fished from the drum for her she said, "Rena—you're not proposing to stand in for Roddy all night, are you?"

The green eyes above the mask were defiant. "Why not?"

"Just—because it's so unnecessary. If Mac really isn't fit there are plenty more of us. You're such a glutton for punishment."

"I'm a glutton for experience, my dear. Remember, I've my Fellowship coming up soon. I'd hate to miss it."

When they moved over to the table Staff Haggerty turned round from her trolley and began to prepare ligatures on the side table. She blinked her colourless lashes and said, "Good evening, Miss Bromwich."

"Evening, Staff. Is this a male or a female?"

"Neither. It's a child."

And that, Vivien thought, would be the story of the week, when Rena repeated it in the common room. Rena was laughing under her mask, and the theatre pro's eyes flickered. "I see, Staff, thank you."

"Like kittens," Rena murmured. "You can't tell until they're weaned." She raised her voice. "It's a boy—I've just examined him."

Staff Haggerty was well aware that they were laughing at her. She finished threading a needle and set it neatly on the trolley with its little hank of suture. "What I meant was that you needn't bother about the bed-state, Miss Bromwich. The children's ward's practically empty: they've only just opened again after decorating."

She nodded to the pro, and then the ward nurse came thrusting backwards through the double doors dragging the trolley behind her. Vivien took her place opposite Rena

12

and reached for the towel-clips. There was a job to do, and there would be no more talking until it was finished.

*　　*　　*

When she got back to the Nurses' Home afterwards, Johnny was dancing with a moonlight blonde, with size two feet and eyes like a Persian kitten. She was delicious, and she danced like a dream, and Vivien had never seen her before.

Johnny winked broadly as they passed, and at the end of the slow foxtrot he brought his partner back with him. "Viv—I don't think Bill Stedman was exaggerating! Sister, this is Miss Bromwich, Mr. Malcolm H.S. Sister Paulson, Viv. She takes over theatres tomorrow."

The girl's grip was astonishingly hard. "How do you do, Miss Bromwich? I expect we shall see all we want of one another tomorrow."

Her voice was as soft as Irish mist and she was almost too feminine to be true, Vivien decided. Except for that revealing handshake.

"Yes, I expect we shall. There's quite a list. Still some holiday backlog, that's the trouble."

Sister Paulson smiled gently. "I'm sure we shall get through all right. Sister Blount tells me he's a bit of a hustler."

"I wouldn't say he hustled. Very tidy, and quick. The smallest incisions in the world."

"Good. So much less shock for the——" She stopped, and her great kitten eyes were laughing. "Dear me, we're talking shop. Sorry!"

"We began it," Johnny assured her.

"Well, will you excuse me? I promised the next waltz to Mr. Stedman. I think"—she lowered her voice, "it's the only dance he's sure of!"

They watched her go, and smiled over Bill's struggles to keep pace with the band. "You can almost hear him saying, 'ONE-two-three', can't you?" Johnny said. "Poor old Bill. If he's going to do much of this we shall have to give him some lessons."

"He won't have the chance to do it very often. Wait till the students see her!"

13

"Darling, theatre sisters do not hob-nob with mere students. For them there are the junior pros, bless their bewildered little hearts."

He steered her out on to the floor. "I wonder," Vivien mused, "what female registrars are supposed to hob-nob with?"

Johnny looked down at her quickly. "You're really bothered about Rena, aren't you?"

"It looks such a lonely job, from here."

"Maybe. But she chose it, remember. She could have gone out into practice, or specialised in gynae., or something. It's entirely her own idea to make herself more of a man than the men."

"There's nothing very mannish about Rena. That's the trouble."

"Not superficially, perhaps. But deep down inside she always seems to be saying that anything they can do she can do better."

"Well, she isn't happy. Anyone can see that. I wish—"

"Yes?"

"I wish she could fall in love with someone strong enough."

"Strong enough to what? Master her?"

"No, not that exactly. Strong enough to make her feel safe to relax—and to *want* to."

Johnny turned Vivien towards the door. "Here she is."

Over his shoulder she watched Rena sweep in and pause inside the doorway. She hadn't put on the white chiffon. She was hard and bright in a vermilion silk jersey top and a tight black skirt, and her mouth was a savage slash of lipstick behind blue cigarette smoke, as she stood there, tall and square-shouldered, looking over the heads of the crowd.

"How do you know she hasn't?" Johnny said gently.

"Hasn't what?"

"Fallen in love. Could be that's what's eating her?"

At the end of the dance he fetched Vivien a long cold drink, and then went over to ask Rena for a quickstep.

They were laughing as they danced, and they stayed together for the tango that followed. Vivien, sitting alone, was suddenly aware of the man standing in front

14

of her. She had the impression that he had already spoken to her once. "I'm sorry," she said. "Did you say something?"

"I wondered whether you'd care to dance."

His voice was deep and unfamiliar, with a creamy regional drawl. South, she decided. Devon or Dorset perhaps. "Thank you. I can't pretend the tango's my strong point, but I'm willing to learn."

"I'm sure we shall manage beautifully. Shall we try?"

He was not tall, not like Johnny, but he was exactly tall enough to be comfortable to dance with. And he was extraordinarily light on his feet. As delicate as a cat, she thought. And because she was passionately fond of cats she smiled to herself at the thought.

"You were thinking?"

"Oh, nothing publishable. Tell me, where do you come from? Devon?"

"No. Sorry, Dorset. Does it show?"

"Just enough. I detest voices with all their origins squashed out of them. Mass-production standard English. Don't you?" She had not realised she could tango so well. She was utterly caught up and disciplined by the rhythm of the music. It was a *complete* feeling, she thought. No loose ends.

"I think I do. Of course the thing is to be bilingual. Standard English for business and so on, and one's own *patois* for friendly conversations. You're Warwickshire, of course."

"Clever of you. It's not an easy one to pin down. Everyone knows Birmingham and Black Country, but Warwickshire's more countrified altogether."

He piloted her through an intricate variation which demanded all her concentration, and at the end of it she was conscious of Johnny's surprised face over Rena's shoulder.

A moment later Rena had left the floor and was hurrying through the garden door with Johnny shouldering his way through behind her. Vivien wondered if there could be another emergency call. If there was, why had she not been told? Had Johnny gone in her place?

When the urgent music came to an end she sat down, and her partner said, "I'll get you something to drink, shall I? You must be hot." He reappeared with a mist-frosted glass in a matter of seconds. It had taken Johnny much longer, she reflected.

"You must have influence!"

"No. Sheer persistence. Long experience in the Army, actually."

"I see. You're a queue-jumper." He had cat's eyes too, she noticed. Topaz. They were as intelligent and perceptive, in a different way, as those of Sister Paulson.

He went on looking at her. "Which ward are you on?"

"Oh—I'm on Mr. Malcolm's firm. Wards Nine and Ten, and a few pirated beds scattered elsewhere."

He fumbled with his cigarette-case, and then, when he had lit her cigarette and his own, he said, "I've—I've dropped something of a brick, I expect."

"Have you? Why?"

He had a wide white smile, and it lit his lean face. "I quite thought you were a nurse. And you're not, are you?"

"I'm Mr. Malcolm's H.S."

He stood up. "You must forgive me. Protocol is a very odd thing. I enjoyed the dance—thank you so much." She saw that he had flushed uncomfortably and wondered why.

"But so did I! Thank you. Does it matter?"

"That you're not a nurse? Not to me. It may do to you."

She frowned. "Look, are you seeing this as a question of status or something? You mentioned protocol. Because if you are, let's have this much clear——" She hesitated, and then, emboldened by the perfect fit of their interlocked glances: "If you could have stayed to chat to a nurse, why couldn't you stay to chat to me?" He was still looking straight at her, but she was sure he was not listening. "We and the nurses are—are a *team*. There's no question of a dividing line, surely?"

He dropped his eyes, and the spell was broken. "No, of course not. It makes no difference to me. But there are things *you* may not do, I imagine. For instance, you can't very well——"

Johnny interrupted him. "Excuse me, old man. Viv, will you go to Rena? She's not well. Says it's a headache, but she wouldn't take anything for it. Go up, will you?"

"Yes, of course. Johnny—this is——" But her partner

16

had gone. She frowned. "That's odd. I didn't see him go, did you?"

"Who? The Tango King? He slid off to the bar, I expect. Who is he, anyway?"

It was with a faint sense of disappointment that she remembered he had not told her his name. Still, if he was on the house she would be sure to see him again, she thought.

"I've no idea. It doesn't matter. I'll go up to Rena. I saw her bolting, and I thought maybe she had another emergency. Johnny—she *can't* take the night calls. Mac's supposed to be first on, and he's off sick again. I'd better tell them that——"

"No, you don't. I've already left *my* name down at the switchboard. Forget it, darling."

*　　　*　　　*

Rena lay on her bed with a cold compress on her forehead.

"You shouldn't have come away from the hop, Viv. I'm all right."

Her head and hands were very hot. "Are you? You'd better let me get you something. What do you usually have—codeine?"

"Usually?" Rena laughed shortly and closed her eyes. "It isn't exactly *usual* to——" She stopped. "I don't often get headaches like this." She pointed to the dressing-table.

There were codeine tablets in a box, and Vivien took out two and drew water from the wash basin. "Take these, Rena, there's a dear. I can't just do nothing."

After a moment Rena's eyes opened again, and she got up obediently on to one elbow and swallowed the tablets. "Thanks. Just clear off and leave me to it. I shan't die or anything."

There were amytal capsules in a brown glass bottle on the bedside table. Vivien picked them up. "You won't be wanting these now." She put them on the shelf over the basin. "Do you often take them?"

"Often enough." Rena's eyes were closed again. Her handsome face was deathly pale. "I'm not the world's best sleeper, Viv. My brain won't quieten down at the end of the day. Still, it's all part of the game, I suppose."

"If it was a game you'd be enjoying it," Vivien told her bitterly. "I don't see what fun you get."

"I'm not in it for the fun."

Vivien sat down gently on the side of the bed. "Then what? If you—if you could clarify it to me, it might not drive you so much."

Rena shook her head slowly and kept her eyes closed. "I'm the one," she said. "I'm doing the driving. Trouble is," her voice was trailing off into sleepiness, "sometimes the other traffic gets in the way. Things you thought you'd passed, you know. . . ."

"I know," Vivien didn't know, but there was nothing else to say. "You'll win out, Rena. Don't worry so much."

Rena turned her face away towards the wall. "Do you know how long I've been at Queen's, Vivien?"

"Tell me."

"Ten years. Including my final year. I—I didn't qualify until I was twenty-seven, you know."

"I didn't know." That makes her thirty-six, she thought. And tonight she looks even older than that. She smoothed back the heavy yellow hair from Rena's temples. "It's a long time."

"It's too long to have it—to have it all undone now."

Vivien got up. "It won't be," she said crisply. "Nothing is going to go wrong. You're over-tired. I'm going now, Rena. And Johnny's standing in for Mac, not you."

She slipped out quietly and let herself out of the Residents' House again into the quiet road. There was a man standing on the opposite side of the tree-lined avenue, looking up at the windows of the house. She saw that it was her dancing partner, and walked across, puzzled, to speak to him.

"Were you—looking for me, by any chance?"

Because he started, and looked at her with his golden eyes darkened by dilated pupils, she knew that he had not been. But he said, "I wondered where you'd gone."

"Oh. I came back to look at a colleague with a sick headache. That's all." She turned to walk back to the block, and he fell into step with her.

"And is she all right?"

"She will be. She works too hard." She looked up at him. " *Are* you on the house, or not?"

"Not," he told her flatly. "Good night." He turned on his heel and left her. She walked slowly on, but it was not until she saw Johnny again, waiting for her in the Home hall, that something clicked into place in her mind.

She looked up, faintly bewildered, at him. "How did he *know* it was 'she', when I only said 'a colleague'? He didn't stay to hear what you told me when we were dancing did he?"

Johnny bent to kiss her. "Does it matter, darling? And I've found out who he is, if it's bothering you." He grinned. "You've made a bit of a bloomer."

"Why? *Who* is he?"

"Wait," he said. "Wait until tomorrow morning, and then you'll know. I only wish I could be there to see your face."

"Oh, *tell* me!"

But he only kissed her again instead, and then took her hand and ran her on to the dance floor for the last waltz. He seemed tall, and a little clumsy, and once he trod heavily on her toe.

CHAPTER II

WHATEVER had upset Rena the night before did not prevent her from being early to breakfast. When Vivien hurried into the dining-room she was in the middle of a heated argument with the R.S.O., Dick Clements.

"Have it your own way," she told him. "But you'll see that I was right. I've collected enough case-histories to prove it."

Dick Clements shrugged. "I won't try to convince you, Rena." He smiled up at Vivien. "A woman convinced against her will is of the same opinion still, or so they say. You'll have to learn from experience."

"Rubbish, Dick! Isn't that just like a man, Vivien? As

though the fact that I'm a woman makes any difference. If I were a man I'd still say the same."

Vivien nodded, and slid into the chair opposite her. "Yes, I expect you would. Are you feeling better?" Rena was a little pale, she thought, but she looked lively enough. Only her voice was a fraction shriller than usual.

"I'm all right," Rena told her casually. "Look, isn't your man doing a splenectomy this morning?"

"Yes. Did you want to see it?"

"I certainly do if he's going to do his new fancy method using the cautery instead of ligatures. In fact"—her rare brilliant smile lifted all the drooping lines about her eyes —"I was wondering whether I could butt in and assist." She shot a glance at the R.S.O. "Don't you listen, Dick. This is purely a domestic arrangement."

Vivien hesitated. "Well, *I* don't mind, Rena. You'd have to ask Mr. Malcolm. It depends——"

"It depends what mood he's in, yes, I know. How soon can you *tell* what mood he's in, though?"

"I can't." Vivien laughed. "Sister Blount's the diagnostician there. I gather it has something to do with what he says when he first walks into the surgeons' room. If he asks for tea, that's good; and if it's coffee, that's bad. And if he wants to get straight on, that's worst of all. The nurses know us better than we know ourselves, Rena!"

"I'm sunk, then. We don't have Sister Blount any more!"

The R.S.O. reached for the marmalade. "I don't think that's going to hamper you, Rena. The new girl seems to have all her buttons on. Easy on the eye, too. I've noticed," he mused, "that if they have good eyes they're usually efficient. Comes of being eloquent with them over masktops, I suppose."

"In that case," Vivien began, "the same would apply to surgeons. I wonder——?" She stopped, and in her mind she saw very clearly the clever topaz eyes of her dancing partner the night before. "Or does it?" she said awkwardly. "May I have the sugar, please, Rena?"

"Does what apply to surgeons?" Johnny pulled out the chair next to hers, and reached across her for the coffeepot. "You can't go making any generalisations about surgeons, if that's what you're doing, Viv. They're artists; therefore they're individuals."

"Artists!" Bill Stedman nearly choked. He put his cup down safely and leaned over to expostulate. "Just carpenters, you mean. Where's the artistry in cutting and stitching things you can *see*? Purely mechanical. Now, when it comes to *medicine*——"

Johnny nodded comfortably. "Yes, that's what I used to think. You'll learn, old boy. Skill, that's the thing. And instinct. What is it, for example, that makes a man decide on a median incision for an appendicectomy? Because he instinctively knows that——"

"That he'll get his big fist in easier that way!" the R.S.O. teased. He stood up. "I'm off. Hope you see your splenectomy, Rena."

"I mean to!"

What Rena means to do, she usually does, Vivien reflected. She has her own way too often—that's what spoils her. How would she react if, just for once, somebody pushed her around? "Come up to the theatre with me," she suggested, "and we'll see which way the wind blows."

"What time do you begin? Ten?"

"On the dot." Vivien pushed her chair in, and squeezed Johnny's shoulder. "Second lunch, I expect," she told him. "I'm going up to the ward now, Rena. See you later?"

She found her white jacket in the changing-room, and stuffed her notebook into her pocket before she took the lift up to Ward Nine. Sister White was half-way down the row of beds, charting the temperatures, and Staff Colley was busy behind screens. A scared-looking junior pro was folding blankets on a theatre trolley outside the swing doors.

Vivien nodded to her. "Good morning, Nurse. What are *you* panicking about?"

The girl sighed, and pushed back her hair into her cap. "I've got to come up to the theatre this morning, Miss Bromwich. I'm plain terrified, I don't mind telling you." She managed a tiny smile. "Is that silly?"

"A bit. We shan't eat you, you know. Sister's told you what you have to do, hasn't she?"

"Oh, yes. It's not that. Only the students were telling

21

me that everyone faints, first time up. I'd feel such an ass——"

Vivien grinned. "I'll tell you a secret, shall I? Students faint, yes. Not nurses. Honestly, I've never known a nurse to faint. Only men. It's true!"

"That's a comfort! Will *you* be there, Miss Bromwich?"

"I expect so."

"Well, if you see me looking like doing anything daft, will you just pull a face or something. Then I'll be all right."

"I will. Not that you'll see much of it under my mask. I'd better wiggle my eyebrows!"

She went on into the ward, and Sister White came up the row of beds to meet her. "There's an addition to the list, Miss Bromwich. Came up from Casualty at six o'clock. You'd like to see her, I expect. The end bed." She turned and rustled ahead of Vivien and pulled back the screens where Staff Colley was working. "Not prepped yet, is she, Staff? Let Miss Bromwich examine her first, then."

The girl—she was twenty, Vivien saw from the case-sheet—lay on her side with one leg drawn up, and moved only her eyes.

Staff Colley gently turned her on to her back. "Doctor's just going to look—won't take a minute." She deftly arranged the blanket.

Vivien read the Casualty H.S.s notes on admission. Acute umbilical pain the previous day; vomiting, followed by pain moving into right iliac fossa. Abdomen tender and rigid on admission. Temperature raised. It looked like a clear case of acute appendix. But was it?

As she gently palpated the girl's abdomen she was looking for something more, she hardly knew what.

"True bill, I should think," said Staff Colley. "Prep for appendicectomy?"

Vivien frowned. What was it Johnny had said at breakfast? Something about instinct making a surgeon choose a median incision. "No, Staff," she said slowly. "Prep the whole abdomen, high as you like, will you? I'm not sure about this." Her searching fingers failed to find the mass she was looking for, but that was not surprising, she told herself, for the muscles were too tense to make palpation

22

easy. She pulled up the blanket and nodded to the girl. "That's all. Don't worry."

"Can't I have something for the pain?"

Vivien looked across the bed, and Staff Colley nodded. "She'll be having her pre-med as soon as I've finished prepping her."

"Good." She leaned over the patient. "Nurse will be giving you an injection that will ease you very soon," she said. "And next thing you know the operation will all be over."

Sister White had gone back to her charting. "I think he's in," she told Vivien as she passed. "Abominable smell of cigar smoke coming up the lift shaft, anyhow." She smiled. "That means it's one of his good days, doesn't it?"

"Does it?" Vivien looked blank. "I don't know how you people notice all these signs and wonders!"

Sister White winked at her. "Oh, yes. If he's in his hoity-toity mood, as the nurses call it, he has a cigarette in a holder. If he's on to a cigar as early as this it means he's got used to the day, and he's fairly pleased with himself." She hung up the chart she was holding and walked up the ward with Vivien. "Why, even with the R.S.O. you can tell."

Vivien wondered how. It had never occurred to her that Dick Clements had moods. He was as uncomplicated as Johnny. That was what made him a good surgeon: he was steady. "Can you, Sister? How?"

"Notice his ties, Miss Bromwich. A bow means he's in holiday mood—often wears one on his half-day. And when he's feeling thoroughly put-upon he comes out with his Guy's colours, you know. Makes him feel superior, I expect!" She opened the swing doors and followed Vivien out on to the landing leading to the male ward.

Vivien said mischievously, "And what about me, Sister? Do you observe *me* so closely?"

Sister White twinkled. "Of course. But I'm not going to tell you, or you'll be faking the evidence; and then where shall we be? We like to know where we are, you know, same as you do."

She left Vivien half-way across the flat, when Sister Jones came forward from the male ward. Sister Jones was a small, excitable Welshwoman, and she was in her usual list-morning flap, Vivien noted.

"Really now, Miss Bromwich, you're very late, aren't you? And I'm just off to Matron's office, so I'm not doing a round with you. Staff will see you, if you'll excuse me." She fluttered off down the stairs and Vivien went on into the ward. The staff nurse was showing the junior pro how to make up an operation bed. "And put the hot bottles in before you go to lunch." She turned to Vivien. "Good morning, Miss Bromwich."

"Good morning, Staff. Anything you need me for, befor I go up?"

"I don't think so. . . . Oh, did you remember to order the blood for that gastric? He was grouped on the medical side before we had him, so I didn't think to list him."

Vivien consulted her notebook. "Hales, wasn't it? Yes, I did. Four pints. It'll be up in the theatre, I expect."

"Oh, good. Sister was flapping about it—you know what she is on Thursdays." She smiled. "She goes round in small circles. Funny, the rest of the week she's as calm as the next man."

"I know. She gets awfully keyed up. I don't know *why*. After all, she doesn't have to do the ops."

"Just as well," Staff Roberts said drily. "Men are tricky enough, but if we had——" She stopped, and blushed. "Oh, I'm sorry! I didn't mean that."

"I don't mind if you did, Staff. I've no intention of becoming a surgeon. General practice is the summit of my ambition. It's all right for those who have a vocation for it. Like Miss Todd, for example. She's a born surgeon."

"I wouldn't have said so," the staff nurse commented. She pushed two X-ray forms across the desk for Vivien to sign. "You'll want these to go down today, I expect? I wouldn't have said so. I'd have said she was suffering from frustrated mother-instinct, frankly. She likes doing things for people, doesn't she?"

"I suppose we all do. You too, Staff. Or we wouldn't be here at all." She signed the forms and slid them back across the desk. "I must go. Sister White says she smells cigar smoke!"

"Should be an easy session, then." She held the door for Vivien. "Not like last week."

Vivien rang for the lift, and remembered the previous Thursday. Mr. Malcolm had been in what Sister White called his hoity-toity mood, with a vengeance, and everyone had known it. Even Sister Blount, who was practically unruffleable, had remonstrated with him when he demanded a third swab-count just to keep the theatre pro on her toes. He had complained, too, that the knives had not been properly ground, and said that it was time the Management Committee looked into the way the technicians did their work. One of the porters had given notice afterwards, she recalled, because he had been upbraided about the condition of the hydraulic apparatus of the table. Nobody except Mr. Malcolm had been able to find any fault with it—until two days later when it had suddenly failed.

But it was all due, after all, she told herself, to his passion for efficiency. And obviously some instinct had told him that the table was due to go wrong. Surgeons were not just the carpenters Bill had termed them, she decided. They had to be as observant in their own field as the nurses seemed to be where the staff were concerned.

She looked through into the main theatre as she began to scrub her hands. Mr. Malcolm was already busy at the next sink, and he grunted when he saw her and then took no further notice of her as he methodically scrubbed and rinsed, giving himself ten minutes by the clock on the annexe wall. It seemed queer not to see Sister Blount's bulky figure hovering round the instrument trolley. Sister Paulson moved about so much more lightly, and her kitten-eyes were cool and alert between her turban and her mask. She had small, deft hands, Vivien noticed. She remembered their strength too.

"Blount's gone, then?" Mr. Malcolm said. "New girl seems all right."

"Yes, sir. I think she will be very good. Oh—sir, the splenectomy. . . ."

"What about it?"

"Miss Todd was wondering——"

He wandered away from her with his arms outstretched,

and Nurse Grover fished for a sterile towel and opened the gown-drum. As she tied his tapes he looked back at Vivien. "Wondering what? Whether she can assist, I suppose?" His round red face creased in a smile. "That girl! All right—that is, if you don't mind letting her in on it." He held out his mask tapes for Nurse Grover to take, behind him. "Coming up third, isn't it?"

"Yes, sir."

"Let her know, then. She's not to keep me waiting, mind!"

"No, sir. I'm sure she won't." Vivien caught the junior's eye. "Nurse, would you please ring Miss Todd, and say that Mr. Malcolm will be glad to have her assist with the splenectomy." She looked up at the red second hand of the electric clock. "Tell her to be up here by half-past, will you?"

"Yes, Miss Bromwich."

"Oh, and Nurse. If the ward pro's in the anaesthetic room now, will you give her a message too? It should be Nurse Simpson, from the female ward. Just tell her to remember what I said. She'll know what I mean."

"I will. It's her first time up, is it?"

"So I gather. That's the point."

The girl's eyes smiled over her mask. "All right. I'll look after her. She can stay in, if she likes, and stand by me, instead of waiting outside."

"That would be nice of you, Nurse. Thank you." Vivien began to dry off her own arms with the towel Nurse Grover was holding out at the end of the long forceps. "Six and a half gloves," she whispered. "Somebody gave me sevens last time, and I was dropping things."

Two minutes later the appendix girl was on the table, and Nurse Simpson was nervously unfastening the prep bandage before she retired and left the rest to the theatre pro.

Mr. Malcolm, opposite Vivien, looked down and frowned. "What's this?"

Vivien looked at Sister Paulson, and the big turquoise eyes signalled to Nurse Simpson where she stood against the wall in her green "dirty" gown. Nurse Simpson did not react, and Sister's eyebrows came together. "The notes,

Nurse!"

"Admitted as query acute appendix, sir," Vivien temporised, watching Nurse Simpson fumbling with the chartboard. "Usual symptoms. But I didn't feel quite happy about it, so I ordered a more scopeful prep, in case . . ." Nurse Simpson was blundering across to Mr. Malcolm with the chartboard, and in another second she would be touching his sterile gown. "Stay there, Nurse," she said quietly. "Just hold up the notes for Mr. Malcolm to see. Don't come any nearer."

Sister Paulson flashed her a surprised look, but she didn't care. She had promised to see the girl through. Sister wouldn't know that this was her first trip, or she would have given the order herself.

He peered at the case-papers over his mask, and said, "Hm! What else do you expect to find, then?"

"I don't know, sir. I just felt that there might be more to it. Just a hunch, really, sir."

"I see." Mr. Malcolm waved the nurses away from him, and came round the table. "Then supposing you follow your hunch and do this yourself, Miss Bromwich?" He nodded to the other side of the table. "Go on, girl. Get on with it."

Vivien had learned not to argue with her chief. What was more, she knew she was very lucky to have the chance of operating with him there to advise her. She moved round and held out her hand to Sister Paulson, and when the scalpel was slapped into it she poised it over the patient's yellow-painted skin. "Median, I think, sir."

· Mr. Malcolm's eyebrows moved upwards like brown caterpillars. "You do, do you? Carry on, then." He picked up the artery forceps and watched the thin red line coming from the knife. He hung on the the retractors as she went on through the muscle, dissecting her way carefully, looking for something to explain her doubt.

She had clamped and excised the shiny inflamed appendix before she found it. She looked up at Mr. Malcolm, and felt again with her exploring fingertips. "There, sir!"

He moved his hand under hers, and slid his fingers forward. "Yes, Miss Bromwich. You're perfectly right.

If that isn't an ovarian tumour, *and* a big one, my name isn't Ian Malcolm." His eyes met hers as he mapped it out with his fingers. "Most unusual! It certainly wasn't palpable before, was it?"

"No, sir, it wasn't. The abdomen was too rigid."

"Well, well. Your hunch paid off, didn't it? Get on with it, then. Big receiver, Sister. And more clamps."

Vivien's hands were trembling a little by the time Mr. Malcolm waved her away. "All right. I'll stitch the peritoneum for you. Nicely done."

Half-way through the next case he said, "Here. You finish this anastomosis for me. Your fingers are smaller than mine." And when she had completed the circle of tiny stitches and he had clipped them close, he asked, "You going for your Fellowship, Miss Bromwich?"

"No, sir. I wasn't intending to. General practice, I thought."

"Ridiculous! Hands like yours, and you talk to me about general practice. Must be crazy!" He took the suture Sister Paulson held out and frowned over the needle. "You think again, there's a good girl. I shall be wanting a new registrar one day." His shrewd eyes met hers. "Think about it."

"Yes, I'll—I'll *think* about it, sir."

It was immediately after that, with the glow still about her, that she went outside to see whether Rena had arrived, and saw one of the green-gowned theatre porters unloading a trolleyfull of drums, hot from the autoclave.

He looked at her quickly. "Good morning!"

She was surprised that he bothered to speak to her. And then she saw the tawny eyes, and recalled the deep voice with its slight country drawl. She was utterly taken aback. "*You!*" she exclaimed. "But you're not——"

"Oh, yes." He went on swinging the heavy drums on to the shelf outside the stock-room. "I told you I wasn't on the house!"

Sister Paulson, in her long mackintosh apron, came up silently behind her. "Glove drums, please, Featherstone," she said peremptorily. "Miss Todd is in the surgeons' room, Miss Bromwich. She's nearly ready."

Now we shall see, Vivien thought. Now I shall know

whether this was the ghost Rena saw last night.

But when Rena stalked out of the surgeons' room in her apron and gumboots, ready to scrub up in the annexe, the man had gone back to the lift with his trolley and there was no encounter to observe. It was perhaps just as well, she reflected. It would never have done if Rena had been put off just before she assisted Mr. Malcolm.

"You managed it, then?" Rena said. "Thanks a lot. Do the same for you one day."

Vivien followed her into the theatre when the case came in, and stood watching, beside the theatre nurse.

Mr. Malcolm finished what Rena called his "fancy work with the cautery" and looked up at last. "Want to take it from there?" he asked Rena.

"May I, sir?"

He grunted. "Miss Bromwich isn't so backward in coming forward," he said. "Make a fine surgeon one day, that girl. Nice hands. Very nice. Found me an ovarian tumour this morning."

"Indeed?" Rena's eyes were dangerously bright. Why did he have to say that? Vivien thought impatiently. He ought to know how insulting it is to compare me with her. But Rena was saying: "I agree with you, sir. I hope you can persuade her." She looked briefly at Vivien as she said it. "She'll waste herself, if she's allowed to." She tossed the Spencer-Wells forceps into the lotion bowl at her side. As contemptuously as if they were physicians, and men at that, Vivien told herself.

*   *   *

The list went on through the morning, and there was no more talk after Rena had gone away. Mr. Malcolm worked quickly, and Vivien had to be alert to keep pace with him. And all the time Sister Paulson was there, at her elbow, silently efficient, passing instruments and swabs, and anticipating perfectly what would be needed.

At the end of it, it was half-past one, and Vivien was glad to climb out of the hot boots and the sticky rubber apron and have a shower before she dressed again. In the surgeons' room Mr. Malcolm waved her to share his teatray. "Good girl, this new one," he remarked. "Quicker than Blount was.

"Yes, sir. Considering this is her first day we did very well, I thought."

"Shan't keep her long, I expect. Too pretty for that. Just come out of the Q.A.s, she tells me. Wonder they didn't snap her up."

"She's very attractive, yes, sir."

He waved a bitten biscuit at her. "You just think about what I said to you. Wasting your time, working with me, if you're not going to go on with it."

She flushed. "I might get married, sir."

"Any fool can do that. Any fool can keep house. Any fool can go into general practice, if it comes to that, so long as he can write a 'scrip and keep a list of consultants handy. But *you* can do *surgery*. Not everyone's meat, is it?" He looked a little affronted. "Don't you *want* to stay on my firm and take your Fellowship?"

She stood up and set her cup and saucer down on the table. "I—I've just never thought about it, sir. But I will. I promise, I'll think it over."

*   *   *

Everyone else had had lunch and gone across to Out-patients and to the wards, but Johnny had waited for her, drinking a second cup of coffee. "Why the starry-eyed expression, darling?" He reached up and pulled her face down to his. "Old Malcolm been making passes at you?"

"Silly! No, but Johnny, he wants me to do my Fellowship. He—he says I'd be wasting my time not to."

"Oh, tripe, darling! You don't want to turn into another Rena, do you? You've always said——"

She sat down, surprised to find herself feeling mutinous. "I *know* what I've always said. And I still say it. But it was nice of him to be encouraging, wasn't it? It's a change to be praised instead of criticised, after all. Wouldn't *you* be pleased?"

"Yes, but that's different. I'm a man, and I *have* to think about having a career and providing for a family.

Don't I? You don't."

He's too bad, she thought. It was pretty clever of me to find that ovarian, after all. Why can't he let me glow, just for once? It's not as though I meant to take Mr. Malcolm seriously. . . . "I know I don't, Johnny. I was just being childish. Another thing." She picked up her knife and fork. "I didn't tell you. I had my surprise all right this morning."

Johnny frowned. "Surprise? Oh—of course. The Tango King. Yes, I thought that would shake you."

"It did! But surely he's something more than a theatre porter? He can't be a student, filling in for the fun of it, the way they do out of term, can he?"

"Could be. But he's a bit old for that, don't you think? Must be close on forty."

"As much as that?" She poured herself a glass of water. "I'd have said thirty-odd. Johnny—— No, it's silly."

"What is? Out with it."

She frowned, and stopped eating. "Am I crazy, or did *you* get the impression that Rena had seen him before? That that's what upset her?"

"I'd say you were crazy. She does *get* these migraines, you know she does. And she'd had a hard day. Why do you think that, anyway?"

"I don't know. Another of my idiotic hunches, I expect."

"I expect so. You haven't *said* anything to Rena, have you? I mean, she might feel it was a bit infra dig., having her name linked with that of a new porter!"

"Of course not! But if it comes to that, there's nothing infra dig. about it. All sorts of people do porters' jobs these days. He could be anything, from a late student to a writer getting local colour."

"He could be," Johnny said easily. But I don't expect he is, Viv, so there's no need to excite yourself."

Suddenly she was angry. "I'm not exciting myself!" She smacked her hand down on the edge of the table, and managed to upset her glass of water. By the time Johnny had mopped her skirt she was full of contrition. "I'm sorry, darling. I don't know what came over me."

"No," he said mildly. "I don't think I do either. Never mind. No O.P.s for either of us today, thank God. Let's

31

go out, huh?"

She nodded. "Yes, let's."

They spent a lazy afternoon on the river. Already the autumn had gilded the overhanging trees, and there was something melancholy in the air.

"Bonfire smoke," she said, "always fills me with unutterable nostalgia. I can't think why. Does it do that to you, Johnny?" She lay back in the punt and looked up at him.

"Can't say it does." He came to squat beside her. "You *feel* things too much, Viv. Remember what somebody or other said: 'Life is a comedy to him who thinks; a tragedy to him who feels'? You can't go through life on your emotions, love. You'll wear yourself out. Doctors, and doctors' wives, can't afford to be sentimental. If they did, they'd spend all their time worrying about the patients."

"Then I don't think I want to be a doctor's wife."

It burst from her almost unaware, and when she had said it she looked up guiltily into his face.

"I didn't mean——" she began.

"I know just what you meant, Viv." He smiled complacently, and went back to his pole. "What you meant was that your boss's odd word of encouragement has put ideas into your head! What's more, you're the tiniest bit jealous of Rena."

"*I?* Jealous of *Rena?* What utter nonsense, Johnny!"

"Look, are you quarrelling with me?"

Unaccountably she began to cry. "Yes, I think I am."

"Then I'll take you back, and you can sort yourself out before tea. You're tired, that's what's wrong with you." He began determinedly poling upstream, not looking at her.

Men! she thought angrily. As soon as a woman begins to think for herself they tell her she's tired. Tired! If you don't agree with them their pride makes them think you're not in your right mind, so they ask if you feel quite well, or if you're tired.

And then she watched his strong brown arms, and the easy swing of his broad shoulders. She noticed the way his hair grew, fine as a baby's, in the nape of his neck, and she was unbearably moved. "I'm sorry, darling," she told him. "I truly am." She struggled to her knees, and waited for him to bend down to her.

But for once he did no such thing. He simply said, "All right, Viv. Forget it!" and went on rhythmically poling, with his back to her.

*　　*　　*

Rena joined them at tea in the Residents' dining-room. She told Viven, "Of course, Mr. Malcolm was quite right. You *would* make a good surgeon, if only you'd put your mind to it, Vivien. Why don't you?"

She made some noncommittal reply, and Johnny glowered and said, "Please. Not again. We've already discussed this up and down the length of the river." And then his good temper prevailed, as it always did, and he added, "We can't all be as good as you, Rena, so there's no point in competing." He smiled at Rena. "I still think, though, that if you'd settled for a home and a family you might have found it just as satisfying as other people's insides, you know."

Rena's eyes blazed at that, but she said nothing, and after he had gone off to his wards she swallowed, and said, "What he doesn't know is that I once *did* settle for a home and family, Viv. Only you're not to tell him that. I don't want to tell the world I'm a failure as a woman."

Vivien was startled. "Thanks for telling me, Rena. I had no idea. I—I heard you'd——"

"Lost all my boy-friends to the nurses? That's what they choose to think. Let them. It doesn't worry me. I did have two good friends, I admit—but that's all they were— who subsequently married ward sisters. That's how *that* rumour began. In fact, I pretty well engineered their assignations for them!" She laughed shortly. "I'm—I'm not in a position to have boy-friends, Viv. Odd, but true."

"I'm sorry. I—I just didn't know."

"How could you? I've told you, nobody has ever known. I don't know why I'm telling *you.* Only that the time comes when you have to talk or bust, I suppose. And I don't think you're a gossip."

"I won't tell a soul." Vivien reached out to touch Rena's

arm. "I'm sorry things went wrong, Rena. But there's nothing I can do, is there?"

"Not a thing." Rena poured herself a second cup of tea. "Not one single thing, my dear. Forget it."

Again she thought of Featherstone, with his strange, golden eyes. "Was he—was he a doctor, Rena?"

"Oh yes! A very good one too. Or so I thought."

That settled it, then. No doctor would be playing student, or filling in with portering jobs. Her imagination had been playing tricks with her. Johnny had always said she was too imaginative. Could be he was perfectly right. He often was.

CHAPTER III

TWO days later, on Saturday afternoon, Vivien had her first real quarrel with Johnny. It was all about nothing, and she knew it, nevertheless she was unable to prevent herself from carrying it through to its obvious conclusion.

When Johnny, whistling ominously to himself, had stalked out of Casualty and left her to finish alone the plaster over which they had disagreed, Sister Bedderidge came forward from the background and helped her. "What was all that about, I wonder?" she asked in her motherly way. "*Not* like Mr. Dysart to take offence like that, is it?"

"My fault," Vivien told her. "I ought to have let him do it his way. But I got the bit between my teeth—you know how it is."

"I know." It had all been so very civil on the surface: there was nothing to tell the patient that "the lady doctor and the big one" had disagreed. But Sister Bedderidge had not been running Casualty for twenty years without knowing how doctors ticked. "Never mind," she went on, as she squeezed out the last bandage from the slopping bowl. "We all have our different ideas; but between you and me, Doctor, it doesn't amount to a ha'p'orth of difference in the end result." Sister Bedderidge called everyone 'Doctor'—even the finals-year students—because she said it gave the patients more confidence. "All this Miss This and Mr. That," she used to say, "makes the patients think you're not real doctors at all."

"I suppose you're right," Vivien admitted. "I ought to have given in."

"Yes, well, if there's any giving in to be done, I always think it's best to let the men have the last word, Doctor. They set a lot of store by it. Women know when they've won, and they don't need to have it in black and white the way men do."

Nevertheless, she did not apologise. She longed to, when she saw Johnny's miserable face at the supper table. Sister Bedderidge was right: it was quite unlike him not to bob up again at once. But her pride reminded her that she had been in the right: Mr. Drood *did* like his hip spicas done her way, and not his. Mulishly she made no attempt to heal the breach, and he went out without her for his evening stroll for the first time in six months.

The R.S.O. said, "What's biting Dysart?"

"My fault," she confessed. "We argued over one of Mr. Drood's spicas in Casualty. He said 'I was always perfectly right', in the kind of voice that meant I was being abominably bossy. I *know* I ought to apologise, but——"

"Oh, why should you? You've worked with Mr. Drood on occasion; he hasn't. Let him sweat it out, Vivien. You spoil him."

Bill Stedman looked up a little shyly, and suggested, "Would you like me to—to try to smooth him down? He looks awfully dreary."

"No, Bill. Nice of you, but it's my job. I expect I shall get round to eating humble-pie before the night's out."

Only she didn't. The week-end passed with Johnny avoiding her with elaborate care; and with her too proud and angry to do anything about it. And on Monday morning, fretfully searching, as she so often did, for gumboots that would not swamp her, she walked into the theatre linen-room without knocking.

The door met with some resistance, and when she jerked it sharply Johnny marched out with a smear of

Sister Paulson's distinctive cyclamen lipstick at the corner of his mouth. He went straight down the corridor without speaking to her, but Sister Paulson took her time to rearrange her theatre turban and said sweetly, "Oh, Miss Bromwich! Looking for your little boots again?" It was exquisitely done, and Vivien could not have felt smaller or more foolish.

"I was," she said. "And I do think you might see that they are kept in the surgeons' room, or in the annexe. It's a perfect nuisance having to keep looking for them."

Sister Paulson looked down at her own small feet, and said, "I'm so sorry. I keep calling them 'my' boots, you know. I always forget they're yours."

The R.S.O. heard the tail-end of the conversation from the corridor, and put his head in and said, "For heaven's sake, Sister, can't you put in a requisition for some more boots? *I* can never find any *big* enough. It is your job, after all."

And walking through to the annexe with Vivien he told her, "It's not working out so well as I thought it would, after all. That one's remarkably obstinate when she likes." He grunted, as he began to scrub, "Why *can't* women be more co-operative?"

"If you mean me," Vivien told him, "I *am* being. If it isn't co-operation to slop about in size sevens, I don't know what is. *Her* boots indeed!"

Dick Clements grinned at the nailbrush. "There, there," he said. "All better now. But if she doesn't damn well order some more boots I'm going to want to know the reason why, all the same."

And later, in the common-room, he told Bill Stedman, "You needn't think those big eyes mean anything, Stedman. A more prickly woman I never met. I don't know how you fall for that sort of thing."

"I don't, really," Bill confessed. "Only she was a stranger, and I thought someone ought to ask her to dance. And she really was *quite* nice to me, you know."

"Of course she was," Rena cut in unexpectedly. "Why shouldn't she be? I'm sure you put yourself out a good deal to entertain her."

Bill looked back at his notes and blushed. "I'm afraid

she found me rather dull," he said. "Women do. I can't make their sort of conversation."

"Maybe not. But you have a very comforting bedside manner," Rena told him, "and that's what counts in the end."

"*Have* I?" He stared.

"Of course you have. And you know it," she said shortly. "And isn't it time you were thinking about your Membership?"

The R.S.O. said, "My dear Rena, he's *been* thinking about it. For at least five years, to my certain knowledge. But that's as far as it gets."

"With a brain like yours," she grumbled, "you ought to be ashamed of yourself, Bill."

Vivien said, "He's like me—he finds it easier to vegetate."

"Better not let Mr. Malcolm hear you say that," Rena warned her. "I've assured him you'll rouse from your apathy and decide to go on with surgery."

Vivien thought of Johnny, and said, "Well, you never know. I might, at that. Trouble is, Rena, I don't know myself what I want to do. My feelings are a bit mixed, right now."

By the time she went to bed—without seeing Johnny—she had almost made up her mind. She knew, foolishly, that it was the smear of lipstick that had brought things to a head, and she was furious with herself. It was probably her doing, she reminded herself. Anyone can make a man kiss her if she wants to. For a mad moment she was overcome with an impulse to play *quid pro quo,* and then her sense of humour came to the rescue. Imagine me, she thought, flinging myself into Dick Clements' arms to make Johnny jealous. Johnny would probably only laugh, and she knew it.

* * *

The next afternoon she took the Old Patients' clinic for Mr. Malcolm. He had so many outpatients that he had to have two days for them—old patients on Tuesdays, and new ones on Thursdays. He invariably turned up in person on Thursdays, but as often as not Tuesdays were left to her and Roddy MacBain, since they were mostly routine follow-ups and didn't require to be diagnosed. Mac was back on duty again, still sniffling a little, and Vivien said, "Look, Mac, there are an awful lot of children in the queue today. Their mums will only fuss about them catching your cold; and they'll be right. You go off, and I'll cope."

He peered out gloomily into the waiting hall, and came back again. "Yes, you're right. Babes in arms and whatnot. Will you really? I'd be grateful. Maybe there's something I can do for you instead?"

"No, I don't think so. I'll tell you when there is. Stand in for me one night, perhaps?"

"Surely. I'll do that. Just say the word."

"I will." It may come in useful some time, she thought. Who knows? I may be glad to take him up on it one evening.

She and the clinic nurse waded slowly through the queue, as they came in one at a time to the consulting-room. There was nothing much to do for any of them, except to look at old wounds, write up dressings and lotions, and advise on massage and physiotherapy. It was rather dull. And then a follow-up fracture case came in, a girl of about fourteen, and Vivien, turning to examine her, stood still for a moment.

The thing to do, she decide, was to focus the child's attention on her injured leg, and she took her time examining it while she simultaneously listened to the girl's breathing and watched the irregular movements of her chest.

She stood up at last. "Notice anything, Nurse?"

"Yes. Irregular resps. *And* athetoid movements."

"Good girl." It was such a joy when they really took an interest. "Implying?"

"Early chorea?"

"*I* think so. Ask Mr. Stedman if he can spare a moment, will you, Nurse? And I'd like the mother in now."

The girl was watching her as nervously as a startled pony, with her eyes rolling and showing their whites. Typical, Vivien thought. She said, "All right, Muriel. I just want another doctor to look at you. Nothing to

38

worry about."

The R.M.O. himself came in, not Bill Stedman. "You want us?" he asked.

"Yes, Dr. Palmer. I'd be glad to have my opinion confirmed on this. Would you mind?"

He held the girl's hand in his and looked her over closely, and then turned to the mother. "Been a bit clumsy lately, has she? Been dropping things, and all that?"

"Oh, she *has,* Doctor! I said to her only yesterday, I said, 'If you break one more cup,' I said, 'you'll——' "

"Yes, yes. Any history of heart, Miss Bromwich?"

"No, not in our records."

"I see. Well, Mother, I think we'd better have Muriel in again. No, it's not her leg. It's what you'd call St. Vitus Dance. Nothing to worry about—but she needs a long rest."

The little woman's face crumpled. "But *Doctor*! It can't be! She's as right as you or me. Never been anything mental in *our* family."

The R.M.O. didn't flicker an eyelash. "I'm perfectly *certain* there hasn't. My word, no! Matter of fact, it's usually the most intelligent children who suffer in this way. You mustn't let it upset you. She'll be perfectly all right again when she comes home. Expect you've thought she was acting a bit oddly, hm?"

"Oh, we have, Doctor. And so irritable! Cries if you look at her, lately."

"Yes, well, that's all part of her condition. We want to put her to bed for a few weeks, so that we know she won't harm her heart, that's all."

"A few *weeks?* But how many, Doctor?"

He shrugged. "Hard to say. Could be three months, but we hope not. At least a month, I'd say."

"Oh, but she's got her exam to take for the Tech. What about that, Doctor?"

"I'm sorry."

When the mother had gone home to fetch nightgowns for her daughter, Vivien said, "Have you been worrying about this exam, Muriel?"

The girl tried to nod, and succeeded in jerking her head violently. "Don't—want to," she got out.

39

"You don't want to go to Technical School? Is that it?"

Dr. Palmer glanced at Vivien and nodded. "There you are, you see? You can talk about rheumatic infection until you're blue in the face: I shall still say psychomatic stress." He patted Muriel's shoulder. "If you don't want to, you don't have to. You enjoy your holiday.' '

Her mouth twitched wide, and snapped back again, in the typical choreic *risus*. Somebody was on her side, and she knew it, Vivien thought. Why do parents push their children to this point? she wondered. If I had children —— But that was not a profitable line of thought. "Who was it," she asked the R.M.O., "who said that good teachers all see a little placard over every child's head, saying: 'Don't push!'?"

"I don't know. But it's an excellent thought. Well, I'll fix her a bed in Four. All right?"

"Thank you. I hope I haven't delayed you?"

"Not at all." He waved his hand depreciatingly as he went. "You were quick on that. Nice work."

"Oh, her pulse, and her resps gave it to me. It was pretty obvious.' '

"Some people," he said pointedly, "would have missed it, my dear. Particularly in a surgical clinic." He nodded, and let himself out.

*　　　*　　　*

At tea-time Johnny got up and left the dining-room as soon as she sat down. Dick Clements looked daggers at Bill Stedman and said, "You tactless ass!"

Vivien blinked. "What have you been doing, Bill?" She reached for the toast. It was hard and cold, but she was hungry. "Have you been baiting Johnny?" How can I talk of him so lightly? she thought. But I can't let them see. . . . "What has he done, Dick?"

Bill's face was crimson, and he didn't meet her eyes. "I only remarked that it was a pity you weren't on the medical side," he admitted. "The R.M.O. said that you seemed to be a red-hot diagnostician, and what were you doing in surgery. That's all."

"That's all!" Dick Clements echoed. "And quite enough, too."

Vivien felt her own face burning. "Oh, Bill! How silly of you. Any fool can diagnose a chorea, I should hope."

"Any fool except me," Bill agreed. "That's the point. I missed one last week, and he knew it."

"Local girl makes good," Dick put in. "And then they say woman's place is in the home. Dear, dear!" He got up heavily. "And mine is in Ward Nine."

Vivien looked up quickly. "Ward Nine? Anything wrong?"

"Not to worry. Your ovarian girl's shooting a temp. I said I'd go up. You get on with your tea, I'm sure you've earned it."

"I'd better come up with you." Vivien started to get up from her chair, but Dick pushed her back firmly.

"You'll do no such thing. I'll cope, thanks. Or don't you think I'm capable?"

"Of course, but——"

"Then leave me get on with it! Heavens, girl, you're beginning to be worse than Rena. Preserve me from indispensable women!"

When he had gone Vivien looked across at Bill. "Did I *sound* indispensable? I only meant that it was my case, and that if there was anything wrong it was up to me to put it right. That's all."

"I know. So does Dick. He was only teasing. You rise too easily, Viv. As to Rena—well, she pretty well *is* indispensable, isn't she? So she has a right to act that way." He flushed. "Or I think so."

"She's good," Vivien agreed. "Awfully good. If I were as bright as she is I'd show off twice as much. You must admit there are some dumb types in the profession, compared with her."

"Yes. Mac, for example."

"Mac? I wouldn't call him dumb, exactly. A bit lazy, perhaps."

"Oh, he knows his job all right—and so he ought, with Sir Roy for a father. Trouble is, he can't be bothered to do it half the time. Any excuse to go off sick, or to get

41

people to stand in for him. . . ."

"Too much money," Vivien diagnosed. "Pass the teapot, please, Bill. He knows he hasn't to work to live in comfort."

Bill came round the table and poured her tea for her, carefully. "Probably. Whereas Rena has to stand on her own two feet. So do I. So do all the others."

"No incentive," she agreed. "But he *is* a good doctor, Bill."

"Who is?" Rena came to sit next to her, pushing back her heavy hair from her tired face. "Lord, I'm weary! Who's a good doctor?"

"Mac," Vivien told her.

"He makes me sick!" Rena sounded bitter. "If I had his advantages, where wouldn't I be? Look at him—a father who's one of the finest surgeons in the country; a mother who's one of the best anaesthetists; money galore behind him. And all he does is slack."

"But it isn't his fault," Vivien pleaded. "It's having all those things that makes him idle. He hasn't any real incentive to get on. Not like you."

"Me?" Rena toyed with her teaspoon and laughed shortly. "I'm beginning to wonder whether all my incentives haven't gone for a Burton lately."

"I wish they *would*!" Bill jerked out surprisingly. "We might see you in your true colours then." He stood up awkwardly and went to the door. "I'm sorry, Rena, that sounds rude. It wasn't meant to be."

But Rena said nothing. She only looked after him wonderingly. A little later she said, "Viv, have you and Johnny quarrelled? I don't want to probe—but you used to be pretty close, one way and another. What's the issue?"

"Oh, just a lot of little things that have piled up. Nothing, really."

"I see. I did rather wonder whether—— Oh, leave it."

"Whether what, Rena?"

Rena swallowed the last mouthful of her sandwich before she said any more. "All right—I'll stick my neck out. Whether perhaps he wasn't just a wee bit too friendly with Sister Paulson."

"It's—it's no business of mine if he is," Vivien began.

And then, willy-nilly, she found herself telling Rena a good deal more than she had meant to.

"So? Well, of course, that beastly purple lipstick of hers is quite unmistakable. And if it's any comfort to you, he isn't the only one who's sampled it."

"Who, Rena?"

But Rena shook her head. "No, let it go. Suffice it to say that he isn't. Let's not degenerate into a sewing meeting; this is supposed to be a household of responsible people. I loathe gossip really. It can—it does so much damage."

And she was not to be drawn any further.

*   *   *

Later, when Vivien was about to do her last ward round, Dick Clements rang through to the common-room. "That you, Vivien? Look, we'll have to get this lassie of yours into the theatre again, I'm afraid. You'd better come up."

"I was just on my way. How is she? I've been worrying about her, but you told me to keep out, so I did."

He sighed. "Not *too* bad. But I don't like the wound much. Discharging since I put a probe into it. We'd better get a drain in."

"Damn. I'll come straight up, Dick."

"Yes, do that," he said. His receiver clicked down.

*   *   *

The girl had the beginnings of a roaring peritonitis. When Bill Stedman nodded from his anaesthetist's chair, Dick Clements methodically cut down through the old wound. Sister Paulson passed Vivien a receiver and swabs as green pus oozed to the surface. "Not nice," Dick said.

"Now how did *this* happen?" Vivien wanted to know. "Just my luck! And I was so careful!"

"Not your fault, girl. Just one of those things. She's landed an infection somehow, and that's that. Tie that off, will you, while I clear out the cavity."

Vivien obediently ligatured the bleeding point he had indicated, and watched his long, sure hands at work. "Will she do?" she asked anxiously. "I dread telling Mr. Mal-

43

colm if this goes wrong."

"She'll do. One of those nice little rubber drains, please, Sister. The corrugated ones."

Sister had it ready almost before he asked. "I hope you don't imagine this was a theatre infection?" she said coolly.

Dick looked up. "I didn't suggest anything of the kind, Sister. Believe me, if I thought there was any slackness in the theatre I should go straight to the H.G. Surgical uncleanliness is one thing we can't afford. And I may say," he added, as he tied off the next stitch and shortened the drain, "that our record of airborne infections in this hospital is extremely low. I should regard any increase with the utmost suspicion."

Sister Paulson said nothing, but her eloquent eyes were not pleased. She raised her eyebrows as the theatre pro came in and stood behind her, and leaned back to hear what she had to say.

She nodded, and then turned to Dick. "There's an emergency, Mr. Clements. Perhaps you could have it up right away after this?"

Vivien put the dressing on, and Nurse Grover brought a manytail bandage and helped her to put it on, while Dick stood back, pulling off his gloves. He frowned. "What is it?"

"Head injuries."

He groaned. "Another idiot of a motor-cyclist, I suppose?" Sister Paulson nodded. "I *thought* we'd been remarkably free from them for twenty-four hours. Unnatural. All right—lay it on, Sister. Who's seen him?"

"Mr. MacBain, in Casualty."

"Then I needn't. All right. Twenty minutes?"

He and Vivien dropped their gowns in the bin when the ward nurse had fetched the girl away. "Up on a bed-rest, Nurse Wentworth," Vivien said. "And ask them to watch the dressing and repack if necessary. I'll be along later."

She sat on the arm of one of the surgeons' room chairs and smoked one of Dick's cigarettes, while they waited for Sister Paulson to get the theatre reset. Nurse Grover brought them a cup of tea each, and apologised for the delay. "We've just got to put fresh oxygen on the machine," she explained.

A few minutes later Vivien heard Sister's voice outside. "That's what I'm waiting for, Featherstone. Fix it on right away, please, before we swab down. Nurse Grover—give him a hand, will you?"

Idiotically something somewhere in the middle of her chest contracted, and then relaxed again, merely because she was acutely aware of the sound of Featherstone's light footsteps. She found herself straining to hear his voice, but the doors clicked together on the sound of the heavy cylinder being trundled into the theatre, without his having said anything.

"Penny for them, Viv?" Dick chaffed. "You look miles away."

"I was only wondering—and it's quite irrelevant—what it is that makes people talk about 'broken hearts'. And just which organ *does* produce those queer sensations you feel when you're shocked or thrilled? Because people *do* feel things—here." She laid her hand over her diaphragm. "Corny and platitudinous, but absolutely accurate."

"Some sort of vagus stimulation—or inhibition—I imagine. Sympathetic nervous system working overtime, perhaps. I dunno." He grinned. "Same sort of thing that makes people blush, obviously. Vaso-dilators all up the pole. Why?"

"Oh, nothing. Only you constantly read in books about people's hearts standing still, and so on. And it sounds so absurd. But it really happens." She knew she was chattering to cover up her own unaccountable confusion.

Dick shook his head at her. "Are you telling me that you've only just found out? Didn't your girlish heart ever go pit-a-pat when you were in your teens?"

"I don't remember. No—I can't say that it did. My knees used to turn to water every time our gym mistress smiled at me—that's all. But so did everyone else's, so I expect that was just a herd reaction. Mass hysteria!"

"And what, may I ask, has so belatedly opened your eyes? Don't tell me there's anyone *here* with enough virile charm to set your pulses racing?" He grinned mischievously. "Or have you conceived a tender passion for Mr.

Malcolm since he complimented you?"

"Idiot!" Vivien laughed. "Anyway, he's married."

"He is not! Well, he *was*. Donkey's years ago. A Queen's girl, too. But she died. Since when he's been strictly a bachelor."

Sister Paulson put her head in. "We're ready now," she told them. "And your boots are in the annexe, Miss Bromwich."

"And may they cripple you," Dick murmured. "That's what those beautiful eyes were saying."

They scrubbed and dressed all over again and went back to the table. Bill said, "He's pretty flat, Dick. You'll need to be quick."

"Speed that blood up a bit, Nurse Grover," Dick urged. He watched while she adjusted the tap on the tube from the bottle, and the drips came faster in the glass connection. "That's more like it. Keep it at that, will you?"

The boy was flat, indeed. Every vessel Vivien ligatured slid away from the forceps slackly, and his forehead was livid and clammy.

Dick worked swiftly and neatly, methodically removing bone splinters and clot, and tidying up the mess that was left of a boy's curly head. "How old?" he asked.

Nurse Grover glanced at the case-papers on the side trolley. "Sixteen."

"God! It makes you see red, doesn't it? Letting these babies loose with—with weapons like that. Might as well give 'em atom bombs to play with. Ought to restrict the age up to twenty-five. Of course they ride too fast. Can't blame 'em. I blame the fools who let them have them. Shouldn't be any hire-purchase allowed on them, and parents ought to be prosecuted for giving them as presents."

It was a long speech for Dick. Vivien looked up in surprise. "I agree," she said gently. "You don't need to convince *me*."

Dick bent his head to wipe his forehead on his shoulder, and smiled faintly. "Sorry. My hobby-horse. Had a young brother who nearly killed himself this way." He stood back. "There. I can't do any more now. All right, Bill?"

"Just about."

"Send him down quickly, Sister, will you. Up on blocks, etcetera. I'm going down to the ward myself as soon as I've washed." He plunged out to the annexe and began washing furiously, and Vivien finished bandaging the boy's head and waited to help the ward nurse with the trolley. When she went through to wash herself he had gone.

She realised, quite suddenly, that she had a violent headache. While they had been working she had fought it off, but now that she was free it throbbed with intensity. Somehow she took off her gown and cap, and dropped her gloves tidily in the bin, and washed her hands and arms. And then she stumbled through into the surgeons' room and dropped into the big chair with her head in her hands, still in her sleeveless theatre slip.

"Headache?" Featherstone asked softly, a quarter of an hour later.

She was beyond answering him, and to nod would have been purgatory. But there was no need. He stood behind the chair and drew her head gently back on to the soft cushion he had placed there, and began to run his fingers stealthily through her hair, in long, rhythmic strokes. After she had begun to relax, his hands moved to her neck, drawing the pain upwards and out as though it had been some fluid subject to capillary attraction. She distinctly felt it being drawn out and discarded as, after each long, slow movement, he flicked his hands as if to shake off water.

"Wonderful," she murmured drowsily. "Heaven." She felt helplessly sleepy as the wave of pain retreated before his silky finger-tips and the warmth of his palms comforted the aching muscles of her neck. Obviously he had a gift for that kind of thing, she told herself confusedly. The healing touch.

She had lost all sense of proportion and perspective, and nothing mattered but that he should go on. She was no longer Vivien Bromwich, sitting half-dressed in the surgeons' room, being soothed by the fingers of a theatre porter. She was simply some primitive organism obeying an unreasoning impulse.

And then Johnny walked in.

Featherstone's hands faltered and stopped. Vivien sat

up and blinked, bewildered. Johnny said, "What the hell——?" And then: "Get out!" to Featherstone.

He went at once, but with dignity, and Vivien collected her senses enough to expostulate: "Johnny! He cured my headache! I had the most *ghastly* head, and he——"

But Johnny didn't stay to hear any more, and a moment later Vivien heard his voice in the linen-room, and Sister Paulson's high little laugh.

Furious with herself, and with him, she dressed and went down to the wards. The ovarian girl was doing beautifully, and already her temperature had receded. Nurse Wentworth said, "She'll do now. You can tell. You get a feeling when they won't."

Vivien looked at the pulse chart, and noted the girl's improved colour. "Yes, I think you're right, Nurse."

"I know I am!"

It was good, Vivien thought, when patients had nurses about them who were confidently hopeful, as Nurse Wentworth so often was. Perhaps that was why Mr. Malcolm's women did so well. A pessimist in the ward always seemed to affect the patients badly, she reflected. The worst year for Ward 9 had been when Sister White went on holiday and Sister Branch took over, they said. Sister Branch never smiled, and she always expected the worst; and according to Dick Clements she got it.

She hooked the chartboard back on its rail and went across to the male ward on the other side of Mr. Malcolm's flat.

Sister Jones met her at the door. "Just going to ring for you, I was. Not that you can do anything."

"Is he worse, Sister?"

"The head injuries? No, Miss Bromwich. He died two minutes ago."

Vivien sighed. "What a waste."

"Indeed, yes. And his parents not here yet, either. They sent a police message from Casualty—but they've a long way to come. That's one job I *don't* like, Miss Bromwich, and that's a fact."

"Telling them?"

Sister Jones nodded, and her dark Welsh face was a little tragedy. "Yes. Worrying, they'll be, all the way here—

and then to be told in the end that it wasn't any use."

"Would you like *me* to see them?"

"Indeed not, Miss Bromwich!" Sister Jones drew herself up tall and her dark eyes snapped. "Indeed not, thank you! My job, it is. I'm staying on until they come."

"Thank you, Sister. That's good of you."

"It's what I'm here for," Sister Jones said simply. "Isn't it?"

And what am I here for? Vivien thought, as she went down the stairs. What good did I do? The boy has died, for all our trouble. And all I've done is to make a fool of myself and antagonise Johnny even more.

It would have been nice, she reflected, to be a junior pro, and to be able to retreat to the mattressroom and cry, as they so often did. But a doctor was supposed to be a grown-up person, whatever she might feel.

CHAPTER IV

WEDNESDAY was Vivien's half-day. It had always been Johnny's too; but at breakfast Rena said, "Dick, is it all right with you? I've swopped half-days with Johnny."

"Surely. Edwin won't be in, will he?"

Rena frowned. "I do wish you wouldn't call him that. He's not in the least like anything out of Dickens. Anything but. Our Mr. Drood is an up-and-coming type. No, he won't be in. Not unless he's gone mad. He's playing in the amateur Open, remember?"

"Not *the* amateur Open, surely?"

"Well, the Midlands one. He goes on about his blessed golf until you begin to wonder whether he *is* perhaps an international. Mind you, he's good."

Dick shrugged and smiled. "I couldn't care less. If I need him I shall send for him just the same."

"And he'd come. He's quite capable of asking Sister Paulson for a niblick, instead of a scalpel, in that mood; but he'd come all right."

Bill Stedman giggled, and choked over his tea, and Rena raised her eyebrows. "What's so funny?"

"I was just following the analogy to a conclusion, and trying to picture him playing golf, with Sister Paulson for a caddie, demanding a tenotomy knife to get out of a socket with."

Dick shook his head. "Little things . . ."

But it made a cartoon in Vivien's mind too, and she said, "Yes, and stitching back divots with through-and-through nylon." And then she remembered what Rena had said. "You're swopping with Johnny? But why?" And then she thought, But of course—it must have been his idea. Why did I ask?

Rena hesitated. Then she said, "Well, no secret, actually. Your boss has invited me to tea. Wants to show me——"

"That's what they all say," Dick teased.

Rena ignored him. "Wants to show me his collection of surgical case-histories. Rather nice of him, I thought."

"He *is* nice," Vivien corroborated. "Except when he throws a tizzy, which isn't all that often. And I don't imagine he'd throw one over the teacups."

"If he does," Rena promised, "I shall walk out, with quiet dignity."

The way Featherstone did, Vivien recalled. I haven't seen Johnny since he came into the surgeons' room, she thought. Even if it is all over we ought to do it properly, talk it over. People do. They don't just avoid one another like this.

*   *   *

Sister White was helping Nurse Simpson to raise the ovarian girl up in bed. She nodded to Vivien. "Shan't be a tick, Miss Bromwich. You'd like to look at this, I expect, before I dress it. Screens, please, Nurse."

The wound looked cleaner already, and the girl's temperature was steadily going down, according to the red-lined four-hourly chart. "You feel better?" Vivien asked her.

"I think so, Doctor. Actually, I don't remember much

50

about last night, so I don't know! But I feel more like me."

"Good. She's better have the penicillin again today; and then we'll think about discontinuing it, Sister."

She moved on down the ward. "Anyone else I need see this morning, Sister? Oh—you want me to find you some homers for tomorrow, don't you?"

"I could do with some beds," Sister White agreed. "It's our take-in again tomorrow night, you know. I think Mrs. Jennings would be quite all right to go now. And perhaps Mary Toon? If she comes up to O.P.D. Who else is there?"

Vivien considered. "There's the cyst girl—what's her name?—you know, the neck."

"Miss Albertson," Sister said disapprovingly. "You know, Miss Bromwich, I have to speak to my junior nurses about that. Now don't you go setting them a bad example."

"About what, Sister?"

"You know very well about what. 'The neck,' you say. 'The cyst.' These people have *names*, Miss Bromwich." She smiled to soften the blow. "I remember the bad old days when we called the patients 'number this' and 'number that'. And there are plenty of hospitals still where they're known as plain Smith, Brown and Robinson, with no 'Mr.' or 'Mrs.' I don't like it. It's so discourteous."

"I'm sorry, Sister," Vivien said, genuinely ashamed. "We get into such a habit of calling people 'the appendix' and 'the mastoid' in the house, you know."

"Yes, well, and quite understandable. We do it ourselves. But *not* in the patients' hearing, Miss Bromwich."

"I wish all the other ward sisters felt the same."

Sister White rolled down her sleeves and slipped her cuffs on. "I never concern myself very much with other wards, Miss Bromwich." She twinkled. "I say to myself, 'This is Mr. Malcolm's ward, and here everything must be perfect.' What the other wards do isn't my affair. I have my own standards.". She put her hand on Vivien's arm. "Don't take it to heart, but I can't let *you* do things I don't allow the junior pro to do, now can I?"

"Of course not, Sister. You're perfectly right." She looked down the list of patients in the big report book on

Sister's desk. "I knew there was another for home. There's the—there's Mrs. Godden."

Sister didn't say any more about it. She called Nurse Wentworth. "Nurse, I have to go to the office. Will you look after Miss Bromwich, my dear?"

"Sister *Bedderidge*," Vivien said mischievously, "calls me 'Doctor'."

"No doubt." Sister's eyes were twinkling again. "But I'd remind you that this is a surgical ward, Miss Bromwich. Even when you have your Fellowship, you'll still be 'Miss' here."

"Who said I *was* taking my Fellowship?"

"Oh, a little bird told me." She smiled comfortably and went on her way.

"Sister's little bird," Nurse Wentworth said, "tells her some remarkably odd things at times. It's my belief she sits in the linen-room and makes them up, while she's having her lunch."

"Wishful thinking, eh?"

"That's about it. A little bird told her I was working hard for my Final State—so it must be!"

She examined two more patients, and looked at some of the dressings while Staff Colley had them down, and spent the best part of the morning writing up notes to conclude the homers' case-papers. And at one o'clock it was almost a relief when the telephone tracked her down, and Dick Clements said, "I know it's your half-day, Vivien, but I could do with a hand in Cas. The C.O.'s off as you know, and everyone else seems to be tied up with cut-downs and what-not except Mac, and he's in mid-plaster."

"I'll come straight away, Dick. I wasn't planning anything."

She washed her hands and face to wake herself from the drowse the hour of writing had brought on, and hurried over to Casualty. What seemed like a crowd resolved itself on analysis into two policemen, three ambulance men, and a little huddle of adults on the waiting benches. In the casualty room Dick was coping with a girl's arm, badly cut by flying glass, and there was a man on the other couch with a damp white face and faint, sighing breath.

"Fix that up with theatre, will you? Crush injuries. Doubt if he'll do, but we'll have to try. Group him, Viv, will you?"

She reached for the blood-grouping tray with one hand, and the telephone with the other.

*   *   *

Two hours later she and Dick were in the surgeons' room, getting their breath back and drinking the inevitable tea, dumped on their table by Staff Haggerty, since Sister Paulson had gone off duty.

"Thanks a lot, Vivien," Dick said. "Nasty moment, when that chap's heart stopped."

"You were terribly quick with the massage."

"You have to be!" he said simply. "He'll maybe do now."

"That silence is a dreadful thing, isn't it?"

"Yes. It hasn't happened to me very often, but you never forget it, I suppose."

"No." She put her cup down and sighed. "I think I see now what Rena gets out of it."

"Drama? Power? What?"

She shook her head. "No, none of those. It's—it's a feeling of taking part in something. . . . Part of the infinite. . . . Or does that sound mad?"

"I don't think so. Like watching a baby being born, you mean?"

"That's it exactly, Dick. Part of a—a miracle." She flushed with embarrassment. Dick was no sentimentalist.

He laughed, in a gentle way that meant he was moved but didn't mean to show it. "Audience-participation, the TV people call it. I suppose it's what we all want, to be part of life and not outside it?"

She took a deep breath. "Falling in love with the wrong people, I suppose. All part of the same drive—to be in on things and not get left behind."

Dick got up and patted her shoulder. "I wouldn't know, Viv. I never do fall in love with the wrong people. I didn't think you did, either."

53

"You can tell yourself that it's just a biological urge—natural selection and so on. But is it?"

He leaned on the back of the chair and frowned at her. "Look, Vivien, are you in some sort of a mess?"

"No. I wasn't thinking of me. Why?"

"Well, you've sounded a bit zany lately. And I've never seen old Johnny so cheesed. He used to be the life and soul. And you know quite well you two used to pair off quite a bit."

"I don't ring any bells for him any more, Dick. If I ever really did. Face it—he has other interests!"

"I don't believe that."

"Don't you? She's very pretty; I don't blame him." What a cat I am, she thought. But I can't forgive him for that.

Dick leaned forward and looked straight at her. "What the blazes are you getting at, Viv? *Who's* pretty?"

She nodded at the wall dividing them from Sister Paulson's office. "Isn't she?"

"Well, if you like that sort of thing, yes! But *Johnny*! Are you really serious?"

"Perfectly."

Dick was thoroughly embarrassed by now. "Oh, well. But I find it a bit much to swallow." He moved uneasily towards the door.

"You think I didn't?"

"I'm very sorry, Viv. Anything I can do?"

"Obviously not," she told him bitterly. "You can't control other people's emotions."

"Can one even control one's own?"

"I used to think I could—but I can't. Now what does A do? Let 'em rip?"

He nodded. "If they're constructive, yes. If not, trample on them. That's my formula."

She knew then what she had to do.

There was nothing constructive about dwelling on the effect Featherstone had on her. She had been a perfect fool. The everyday had to take over some time; it wasn't possible to live in that sort of fantasy world, a world of sensuous self-indulgence.

She waited until Thursday morning, when Mr. Malcolm and Mac were scrubbing up before the list, to burn her boats. She stood well away from the basins and said, "Sir, I've thought over what you said. I've decided to stick to it."

It was not one of his good days, but he managed a fairly amiable grunt. "Good. I'll talk to you later. Now get out of my way, there's a good girl."

She did her ward rounds with an airy sensation of new freedom. It was conflict that was the time-waster, she reminded herself. The choice, once made, halved her problems. The glow lasted exactly six hours. Until, in fact, she encountered Featherstone again.

She had left her cardigan in the autoclave-room, so that it would be warm when she needed it. And when she left the changing-room to go over to the Resident's House she slipped in to get it. Featherstone was unloading a batch of drums on to the theatre trolley, and she had to pass him to reach it from the steam pipe. He looked up and smiled slowly.

She was in his arms before she knew that she—or he—had moved. I didn't know people felt like this, she thought, in the last moment of clarity before her senses went down before the onslaught. This isn't how it was with Johnny, this urgency, and not-caring. There was nothing said at all. One moment she was deep in his arms, with her mouth alive under his, and the next he was stolidly clipping drum lids and she was dazedly crossing the floor to meet Rena in the doorway.

Rena frowned. "You all right? You look mighty groggy. Here, put your head down, you ass."

Obediently she put her head between her knees, leaning against the corridor wall. Then she said, "It's so hot in there. . . ."

"Of course it is! What did you go in for at all?"

"To—to get my cardigan."

"Dear girl, I didn't imagine you'd been in to talk to that man." She shivered a little and her mouth tightened. "I was looking for you, actually. Your boss tells me you've decided to go for your Fellowship."

Had she? It didn't matter very much. Not while the memory of Featherstone's touch persisted, like a trembling warmth pervading her very bones. "I did tell him I'd thought about it."

"I'm so awfully glad, Vivien. I'm sure it'll be an immense satisfaction to you to get your teeth into something constructive."

Constructive. That was what Dick Clements had said too.

"I don't know that I'm a very constructive person, Rena. I'm not as ambitious as you, you know."

"Rubbish!" They walked together along the road to the house. "You must get Mac to let you take all the cases you can, from now on. Not that he'll mind; I don't honestly think he *wants* to operate much."

My knees are like cotton wool, Vivien thought. Surely Rena can see that I'm not listening to her? Why hasn't she said anything? "No, I don't think he does. It's just a case of automatically following in Father's footsteps with him. What a change to get over to tea so early—I'm so sick of the usual second-hand, tepid brew."

"Trouble with you is that you're scared stiff of Winnie. Have to be a bit more decisive if you're going to be a surgeon, my girl!"

What would she say if she knew? Vivien wondered. And what's to come of it all? I must be crazy.

But oddly, Rena was looking more relaxed than she had done for quite a time. "How did you get on with him?" Vivien asked.

"Who?"

"My boss. When you went to tea, I mean."

Rena led the way into the dining-room, smiling. "Oh, that? Very well. He had the most marvellous house, you know. On the edge of the hills. He collects animals."

Bill Stedman looked up from the end of the table. "Good, the tea's only just come in. Shall I pour yours, Rena?"

"And mine," Vivien told him.

"Yes, of course. I meant yours too." He jumped up eagerly and slopped milk into their cups.

"That's all I want," Rena said. "Nothing to eat. I'm off out."

"Who collects animals?" Bill wanted to know. "There

56

you are, Rena, I haven't put sugar in this time."

"Thanks, Bill. Why, Mr. Malcolm. He has a huge paddock by the side of the house, and it's full of things he's rescued. You know—circus ponies, donkeys, forest ponies —all kinds of things."

"I never thought he had such a soft heart." Vivien reached for her own tea, and the jam. "He always seems so tough."

Rena was indignant. "Of course he has! He's the kindest man—" She drank her tea hurriedly. "I must be off."

When she had gone Bill said, "But she *never* goes out anywhere."

"Time she did, then. She sticks around her work too much."

"You don't think she's seeing him *again,* do you?" Bill's pale face was concerned, and his eyes blinked owlishly through his glasses.

"I didn't know you cared!" Vivien teased him. And then she looked at him sharply. "Oh! I'm sorry, Bill. I didn't mean to——"

He shrugged and moved up the table to sit near her. "That's all right, Viv. She can't see me, anyway. Just the little fellow who pours her tea, that's me." He smiled ruefully. "No sense in pursuing lost causes, is there?"

"Oh, Bill! If you take it for granted that it's a lost cause——" Then she remembered what Rena had said. Rena had settled for a home and family, once. Rena wasn't free to have men friends—not serious ones. But that cut both ways; it meant that Mr. Malcolm didn't signify either.

And then Johnny came in, with a face like a whipped child. He waited until Bill had made himself scare before he said, "Viv, I'm off tonight. Are you?"

She flushed. "No. No, I'm not."

"Couldn't you—— Oh, well. Forget it." He made great play of cutting a sandwich into neat squares.

But we've got to talk, she reminded herself. We can't go on like this. Some time we have to have it out, once and for all. We've been together for so long. . . .

She said nervously, "I've just remembered something

. . . . Mac owes me a stand-in. He offered to——"

"It doesn't matter." But it did, she could see that.

She rang Mac straight away, and then came back to the table. "He says he'll stay in for me, if—if you wanted to see me."

"*If*," Johnny said bitterly. "I'll collect you in the hall around seven." And then he looked up suddenly uncertain, and added, "All right?"

"All right, Johnny."

Then the others came in and broke it up, and she made conversation about Mr. Malcolm's animals until she could decently hurry out again.

*   *   *

Johnny had Dick Clements' car at the door. "I borrowed it," he said casually. "Easier to get out of town this way."

Vivien sat beside him as he worked his way through the evening clutter of traffic. "That was kind of him."

Other times, when Johnny had wangled the use of a car, she had sat close beside him, with her hand on his knee, or tucked under his thigh on the seat. Now she found herself consciously avoiding contact with him, shrinking to her own side of the car and keeping her hands in her lap. But Johnny didn't seem to notice. Nor did he make any move to touch her.

She threw him a brief glance, and turned away again from his unhappy face. "Where are we going?"

"Home."

"*Home?*"

"Yes, my home. Why not? It's weeks since you——"

"But it's all of thirty miles, Johnny."

"Quite. Hence the car. I have to do a night round about eleven o'clock, if you don't." He smiled faintly. "You know what Night Sister is if she catches us in the wards after midnight."

"She never says a word to *me*."

"No, I dare say not. You don't happen to be a predatory male."

Something wrung it from her: "I sometimes wish I

58

were! There's no fun in being a woman."

That was when it happened.

Her involuntary cry startled him, so that his hands jerked on the wheel half-way round the white line of the bend where the road swung sharply east towards the woods. It would not have been of any consequence had not the noisy singing coach-load of children appeared at the same moment. Johnny, seeing the danger, pulled the wheel too hard towards the hedge, where the new white kerb stood high.

It was the coach-driver who forced the door and lifted her clumsily from the queer upside-down box that had been a comparatively new car. He set her down on the grass verge, his red face anxious and sweating.

"You all right, miss?" He touched her forehead. "Not much of a cut, that ain't. You just set you still a minute."

He plunged back to the car, its wheels still revolving aimlessly above it. When she got her voice back she called, "Is he all right?" and struggled to get up. *Johnny*, she thought. *And it was my fault. I startled him. Oh, God, it was my fault!*

A woman—she looked like a teacher of some sort, Vivien thought—came and waved a green bottle of smelling salts under her nose, "You were going *much* too fast," she said reprovingly. "No wonder there are accidents!"

Vivien stared at her uncomprehendingly. "Is he all *right?*" she repeated. "Please go and look!" She tried again to get up, but the woman pushed her down again. And then she saw the coach-driver's face, coming and going in a red mist as he leaned over her with his lips moving.

"He's hurt bad," he told her. "I'm going to get the ambulance. They'll know how to get him out the best way."

She didn't remember much after that, until she saw Dick Clements' face above her like a great white moon swinging in the sky, and felt the prick of a hypodermic needle. "Just a shot, Viv," he said gently. His voice seemed to be booming in an echo-chamber. "Just a shot, just-a-shot, JUST-A-SHOT. . . ."

✻   ✻   ✻

It was daylight when she sat up in bed in Ward 9's side ward and furiously rang her bell.

Nurse Russell, the senior night nurse, coming running.

"Miss Bromwich? Lie down, now." She pushed Vivien gently back on the pillows and captured her wrist, checking her pulse automatically. "Yes, you're feeling better, aren't you? Could you use a cup of tea?"

"Please, Nurse. What—what happened?" And then the memory surged back and she started up again. "Nurse! Mr. Dysart—is he——"

Nurse Russell kept her eyes on her watch for another ten seconds before she answered. "Mr. Dysart's in Ward Ten side ward. Good thing it was our take-in—it does mean that you're on your own ward." She looked sharply at Vivien. "He's—not in very good shape."

"Tell me, Nurse."

Nurse Russell shrugged slightly, and reached for the chartboard to enter her pulse-rate. "He was in the theatre a long time. The wheel got his ribs, of course, and his head was pretty well cut about, but——"

"But *what*, Nurse?"

"I don't know that I'm supposed to say anything. But I gather it's his hands that are the problem. One of them, anyway."

"His—his hands? But he's a surgeon! His *hands*! How bad, Nurse?" What have I done? she asked herself. What have I done to him?

Night Sister sailed in, with her pale, beautiful face as calm as always, and her hands folded placidly on her belt-buckle. "Good morning, Miss Bromwich. All right, Nurse. You can go."

She sat down beside the bed—a rare relaxation for her—and tucked a tress of hair into the bandage over Vivien's eye, before she said anything.

"You'll be wondering about Mr. Dysart, I expect."

"Tell me, Sister. Don't wrap it up, please."

"He has rib and head injuries; fortunately not as serious as they could easily have been in the circumstances. . . ."

What does she know of the circumstances? Vivien thought. He could have been killed. So could these children.

60

"But his hands, Sister? Nurse Russell was saying——"

"Was she, indeed!" Sister's lips tightened. "His hands. Yes. I'm afraid that though one can be patched up fairly well, the other is rather tricky. Mr. Malcolm had to amputate two fingers, and the thumb is not very satisfactory."

"Mr. Malcolm? *Amputated* two fingers? But—but, Sister!" Vivien held tightly on to Sister's cool, thin hand, and fought back the hot, unreasoning tears.

"Mr. Malcolm, of course," Sister said dispassionately. She gently detached her fingers from Vivien's grasp. "Who would you expect us to get for one of our own Residents? Naturally we rang the senior Consultant."

She stood up, very tall and aloof. "I realise your concern for Mr. Dysart's work, Miss Bromwich. We are all concerned, I assure you."

Vivien laughed bitterly. "*Are* you? He's just 'the hand', I expect, isn't he? He——" She struggled to control herself, and lay down with her hands over her face. "I'm sorry, Sister."

"That's quite all right, Miss Bromwich." Did *nothing* move her? Vivien wondered. "I know you're a little overwrought. Try not to disturb that bandage, please. You've quite a nasty little cut over that eye. We don't want it to leave a scar, do we?"

She rustled away again, her head held high, and closed the door quietly behind her.

When Sister White came on duty Vivien pretended to be asleep. Not that she imagined Sister White would be deceived, but at least she would not disturb her. The nurses came and went, softly tidying the room and twitching her blankets into place, and once the R.S.O. stood at the foot of the bed without speaking and scribbled something on her chart.

It was eleven o'clock when Rena came in. She dumped the morning papers on the bed, and said, "My poor Viv!" as she sat down heavily in the chair beside the bed. "My poor little Viv!" she repeated. "What a filthy experience!"

Vivien let go then, and cried on Rena's shoulder until she said, "Steady on, poppet. I'm drenched!" and patted her back and lent her a big handkerchief. "I know. It's damned tough on Johnny. I couldn't be more sorry. But what can one *do?*"

"Nothing. It was my fault, Rena, don't you see? That's why I feel so ghastly."

"Idiot! How could it have been your fault! You weren't driving."

"I startled him. Just as we were on the bend. He pulled over too far because I startled him. Don't you *see?*" She mopped her eyes, and tried not to lose control again. "And what's worse, Rena, he was trying to make things up—I know he was. He was taking me to his home. I suppose he thought that—that if I went home with him, the way I used to, everything would snap back to normal."

Rena nodded soberly. "But would it have done?"

"No, I don't think so. That's the awful part. I didn't even want to be near him."

"Not even *now?*"

"Only—only because I know I can't let him down. Not now."

Rena shook her head impatiently. "Oh, lord, Viv! *Don't* mix false sentiment with the thing. There have been more unhappy marriages through people's mistaken sense of duty than——" She flushed crimson. "I *know*, you see." She turned her face away awkwardly. "From—from experience."

"You mean—you stuck to someone through it?"

"No." Rena stood up and blinked rapidly. "He stuck to me. Forget it. Only don't make any irrevocable decisions while you're still shaken. It's fatal."

The day wore on after she had gone. Sister White came in and commiserated, and brought in roast chicken for lunch. "Light diet," she said. "I don't think it'll hurt you —do you?" But she was not surprised when Vivien managed only a little of it. "Never mind," she said. "Your tummy's bound to be upset. You were pretty well shaken up, you know. No bones broken, thank goodness, but the R.S.O. says you've to stay here for the present."

When Dick came again himself Vivien said, "I've only just thought, Dick—your car!"

"Oh, don't fret. I expect the insurance people will pay up. Couldn't be helped. Actually, they think it will mend.

It's of minor importance after all."

"I'm so terribly sorry."

"Forget it, Viv. It's done now. I lent it willingly, and I willingly accept the consequences. As for sheer cash considerations, I've told you—the insurance will probably cough up."

Dick didn't mention Johnny's hand, and she didn't enquire. There was nothing he could tell her that she didn't already know. But as he went, he paused at the door and said, "You can get up tomorrow, Vivien, if you feel like it. Run in and see Johnny, eh?" And then he waved and went.

She slept during the afternoon, muzzy with headache, and when she woke there were flowers on her bed table. A great sheaf of red roses that perfumed the whole room.

She had to wait until Sister White came in to say goodnight before she went off duty at half-past six, before she found out who had sent them.

"Did Miss Todd send these in, Sister?"

"I don't really know, Miss Bromwich. There was a note with them. Isn't it here?" She fussed round the room. "I can't see it. Nurse! Nurse Simpson! Where's the note that came with these flowers?"

Nurse Simpson came in and stood frowning for a moment. Then her face cleared. "I remember! I left it in the bathroom when I unpacked the roses."

"Then get it, Nurse!" Sister White shook her head. "Really, that child! She's hopeless."

"She's very young, Sister. And they have so much to remember."

"No more than I had to remember at her age, Miss Bromwich. And in *my* day we worked fourteen hours a day, sometimes more! All for sixteen pounds a year, mark you. That's the trouble these days. What with eight-hour shifts, and all this money, it simply isn't a vocation any more. You don't get the same type of girl at all." She went out to chase up little Nurse Simpson, shaking her head.

When the junior brought the note at last, she said, "I'm awfully sorry, Miss Bromwich. I clean forgot it. You know how it is: I was doing your flowers, and Sister called me to do something else, and when I got back Nurse Wentworth had carried them through for me." She handed over the square white envelope. "Here it is, anyway."

"Thank you, Nurse. And don't let Sister White rattle you. Her bark's a good deal worse than her bite."

She pulled out the single sheet of notepaper.

It all began again....

She read: "*I'm so very sorry. Get well soon. Edward Featherstone.*"

It was in queerly familiar crabbed-looking handwriting, with Greek 'e's and 'd's. Typical doctor's handwriting, she realised. She had been right—he was no ordinary porter.

She lay back and thought again of his silken fingertips on her skin. At least *that* had been constructive. He had used some personal magic to take the pain from her head. If only ... she thought. And then she reminded herself: I've said I'll work for my Fellowship.

And beneath it all she was aware of Johnny, and of what he had suffered through her.

CHAPTER V

AT some time during the night Vivien woke to hear her own screams, and to find Night Sister and Nurse Russell holding her arms as she struggled to climb out of bed.

Panting, she stared at them uncomprehendingly. Night Sister nodded coolly. "That's better. We don't want the other patients to wake up, do we?"

Nurse Russell said, "I'll get her a hot drink, shall I, Sister?"

"Yes, Nurse. And two codeine co. tablets." She took her hands away and rearranged Vivien's pillows. "You were dreaming, Miss Bromwich."

Vivien lay back. Dreaming? she thought. Was that all it was? She was vividly aware, still, of her struggles to escape from the detaining arms of Edward Featherstone while Johnny cried for help from a burning car. She shuddered. "It was only a dream?"

"That's all, Miss Bromwich. Now rest quietly. You're still a little shocked, you know." Sister swept away, and Nurse Russell came back with hot milk and ten grains of codeine and dimmed the light again. But it was some time before her pulse stopped racing and she was able to shrug off the terror that had wakened her.

She slept heavily, and was next aware of what went on around her when Sister White did her morning round before going to Matron's office. "*Not* a very restful night," Sister said. "Or so I hear, Miss Bromwich."

Vivien blinked at her. "No. I was dreaming, I think." She tried to collect her thoughts. "Can I—can I get up now. The R.S.O. said that——"

"I dare say he did. But I'm in charge of this ward, Miss Bromwich, and *I* say you'll stay in bed this morning." She smiled. "Now, you see what it's like to be on the receiving end, don't you? Not quite the same, is it? Never mind. I expect you'll feel steadier by lunch-time."

"How is Mr. Dysart, Sister?"

Sister White pursed her lips. "Another who had a restless night, I'm told. But otherwise his condition isn't much changed." She bent to re-mitre the corner of Vivien's blankets. "You'll see him this afternoon, *if* you rest this morning."

It was a very long morning. Even so, Vivien had not succeeded in marshalling her thoughts when the time came to cross the flat to the male ward. She felt torn and confused, and guilt and concern struggled for priority in her mind. Above all else the thought remained with her: *It was my fault, Johnny's career is ruined, and it's my fault.*

Johnny lay behind screens in the side ward of Ward Ten. His head was a mass of bandages, and one arm, in plaster from the elbow to the finger-tips, lay exposed on a sandbag, raising it for comfort.

Sister Jones whispered, "I think he's asleep. And so he should be, poor soul. He'd a *very* poor night, Miss Bromwich. Only five minutes, mind!"

"All right, Sister. I won't disturb him." She moved over to the bed and looked down at Johnny's pale face framed in bandages.

65

As Sister Jones closed the door he opened his eyes, saw her, and closed them again. "You, Viv." He sighed. "Are you—all right?"

"I'm all right, Johnny. It's you—how do *you* feel?"

"Not very clever."

"It's no use saying I'm sorry, is it? That doesn't help. I *know* it was my fault." She sat down in the chair by the bed and touched his cheek. "Will you ever forgive me? I can't forgive myself unless you do."

"Nothing to forgive." He paused. "I—you'll have to forgive me, Viv."

"For what?" She was startled.

"For what I'm going to do to you."

Vivien frowned. "What *are* you going to do to me, Johnny? Whatever it is, I'm certain I deserve it."

"I wanted to tell you yesterday.... We'd have been alone, at home.... Only we never got there."

"Tell me *what*? Johnny! Tell me what?"

He swallowed, and moved his head uneasily on the pillow. "We—we're all washed up, Viv. It's over. I didn't mean to tell you like this, but that's how it is. I'm sorry."

Now that it had come she felt nothing, nothing but an empty bleakness. "I see."

"Try to forgive me, Viv. I never meant it to go this way."

"Neither did I. Oh, Johnny, I'm sorry I've been so impossible." Now that she was rejected tears of self-pity stung her eyes. "I never meant to hurt you."

He shook his head slightly, wincing as he did so. "You've done nothing wrong, Viv. It—it isn't that."

"No? Then—then you've found someone else, is that it?"

He didn't answer.

"Johnny, if you've found someone else who can make you happy, I shan't argue. But if you're only trying to make it easier for me, I won't accept it." How can I leave him now? she thought. Now, when he needs me. "Tell me truthfully, Johnny—it *is* someone else, isn't it?"

After a long pause he said wearily, "Yes. That's it, Viv. I'm horribly sorry. I—I hope you'll find someone who'll be kinder to you."

"I see." She stood up, and again and hot tears pricked her eyes, so that she had to blink them away. "Be happy, Johnny. That's all I want."

She left him, and went over to the Residents' House. There was simply nothing to say, or to do. It was over. The whole pattern of her life was changed. There was no longer a nebulous future with Johnny, as a doctor's wife, but a long, straight road ahead with the Fellowship at the end of it like a great light. And somewhere in the background, unobtrusively but very definitely there, was Edward Featherstone, and the almost unbearable excitement he carried with him. . . .

Now I have grown up at last, she told herself. Now I begin to live my life the way I want to live it. The way I was intended to live it. Then why do I feel so depressed about it? I ought to be on top of the world. I am free at last to do what I want.

Before the others arrived for tea she walked across to Casualty to exchange her slithering bandage for a strip of plaster. There was still a little queue waiting on the benches outside the examination room, and Dick Clements put his head out as she passed, to call in the next patient. He smiled and nodded to her. "All right, Viv?"

"Thanks, Dick. I just want a neater dressing on this head. I'll get one of the nurses to do it."

"Good show. I'm bows under with this lark." He beckoned to the next man on the bench, and sighed. "Seems Cartwright isn't coming back after all. Know what? He's contracted polio!"

"The C.O.? *No!*"

"True. Ah well, we'll have to manage until the H.G. gets some other mug to take it on. See you!" He waved and went inside and closed the door.

In the dressing-room Outpatients Sister tutted over the cut on her head, and renewed the dressing at once. "Only two stitches," she said. "I don't think it'll be much of a scar, fortunately. You were lucky."

"Yes. But Mr. Dysart wasn't."

Sister's face saddened. "A terrible thing to happen to anyone doing surgery," she said. "But still—maybe it was meant to happen. How do we know?"

"Oh, Sister! These things can't be 'meant'! They're man-made accidents. It should never have happened. It *wouldn't* have happened if——"

Sister opened her large pale blue eyes very wide. "Now, how do you *know* that? No, Miss Bromwich, you don't *know*. You're merely surmising. Not very scientific of you."

"Surely it's scientific enough to see these things as a matter of mechanical cause and effect, Sister? It's no use sentimentalising about Fate. The facts are clear enough—I spoke suddenly and startled Mr. Dysart, his hands jerked on the wheel, and then he pulled over too far to correct the swerve because a coach came the other way. Simple. And my fault."

Sister sighed. "I won't argue with you. But I just don't think it's as simple as that. You've heard about Mr. Cartwright?"

Vivien nodded. "Yes. So we shall be having a new Casualty Officer, I suppose? I wonder whether they've anyone lined up."

"I shouldn't think so—we only had the news half an hour ago. What awful luck, to be taken so ill on holiday."

"Awful," Vivien agreed. "Where is he?"

"Well"—Sister went over to the sink to scrub her hands. "He was on some little island off the west coast of Scotland, I understand. One of these places where the boat calls once a month, you know. No telephone or anything. But the coastguards have a radio, and they sent a message to the mainland, and he was flown out by helicopter to a hospital in Glasgow. Quite dramatic. It's bulbar, you know. The R.M.O. rang up Dr. Palmer and told him they had him into a cuirass in the helicopter, and straight into an iron lung at Glasgow. Otherwise . . ."

"Lucky they have those things so well organised. I suppose people simply used to die before, out on those islands."

"And maybe that was how it was meant to be, too. The world's over-populated, Miss Bromwich. And why? I ask myself sometimes, are we doing right to keep so many people alive? I know it's my job; but, you know, I sometimes look at these puny babies . . . they'd not have been kept alive before we knew about rhesus factor, and so on. And I do seriously wonder whether science hasn't gone too far. Nobody leaves anything to *nature* any more. And you can say what you like, nature's still the best healer. What is it they say? Nature heals and the doctor only encourages the patient while she does it?"

Vivien smiled faintly. "You do too much thinking, Sister. I find your philosophy a bit disturbing. I'm surprised that a nurse should have such ideas!"

Sister's pale eyes blinked. "Oh, I'm not the only one. Even Dr. Jameson said to me, only the other day, 'Sister,' he said, 'I wonder if we wouldn't be better off if the fittest were allowed to survive in the way nature planned?' He said there were too many old people being kept alive bodily who weren't alive mentally any more—and a whole lot more." She folded her towel neatly and hung it up again. "I mustn't keep you. You'll be wanting your tea."

Only Bill was in the dining-room at the house. He poured her tea and asked how she felt. He didn't mention Johnny at all, and Vivien was grateful to him. His "bedside manner", as Rena termed it, could be very comforting. She found herself telling him about the conversation in Outpatients. "I didn't know she did so much thinking," she finished. "I wouldn't have thought she had time."

Bill laughed a little wryly. "Oh, yes. She's told me all that. Oddly enough, you know, I rather think she may be right. There—there *is* a pattern in things, and we do interfere with it far more than we ought at times. We persist in playing God with people's lives." He smiled. "And some of us play the devil with them too, I suppose."

"So you think it would have been *meant* if Tommy Cartwright had just been left to die? How *can* you, Bill?" She hesitated. "And that—that Johnny ought to say 'it was meant to be' when his career is wrecked?"

"I don't know, Viv. At least it's a comforting theory of events." He looked down awkwardly at his plate. "Isn't it?"

"Yes, a comfortable theory invented by man so that he needn't feel responsible for anything that happened—for any havoc he caused!" She was surprised by her own bitterness.

Bill raised his eyebrows "Hey, relax, Viv! We were only making light tea-table conversation, you know."

"Were we? I'm sorry." She got up restlessly to look out of the window. "I'm a bit edgy."

"You should have taken another day or two in bed, old girl. Then we could all have brought you grapes and eaten them ourselves. I was planning to go out and buy you a vast bouquet of roses."

She had left Edward's roses in Ward 9, she remembered with a little shock of recollection. She flushed. "That was kind of you; but now you've been saved the expense." She would have to leave them there now, she supposed. One couldn't very well go back and demand them.

Bill's face straightened. "Oh, lord! Talk of expense. . . . Did Dick tell you about the car?"

"No, only that he thought the insurance people would pay up. Why?"

"I don't know whether I'm supposed to say anything, but he didn't say I wasn't to. . . . Seems they *won't*."

"They won't—you mean the insurance people won't pay? Oh, *no*, Bill! Are you sure?" She swung round to face him. "Did he say so?"

Bill nodded. "He had a phone call from them first thing this morning, and the air was blue for a few minutes afterwards, I can tell you. Seems that he hadn't read his new policy properly, and he wasn't covered while Johnny was driving. Only if he drove himself. And Johnny wasn't insured, you see: he only had a driving license."

Vivien sat down heavily. "But it was pretty well wrecked, Bill. How—how much will it cost to put right?"

"The garage had estimated close on a couple of hundred! In fact, they said it was a write-off really, and he really ought to sell it at scrap price and get another with the insurance money. Only there won't be any insurance money, by all accounts. Rough luck." He added, "I don't suppose Johnny's got that much to spare."

"I'm sure he hasn't. Does he know about this?"

"Heavens, no! Don't say a word, Viv, will you? Dick was *most* anxious that he shouldn't be told. You'll land me in awful hot water if you tell him. You won't, will you?"

"No. I won't. But we can't let Dick stand it. I shall have to—to think of something." But I haven't that much

70

money in the world, she thought. And I can't expect Mother to lend it to me: she hasn't any to spare out of what Father left. What shall I do? It was my fault.... I'm responsible.

Later, in her room, she racked her brains to think of a way of settling Dick's problem. She thought until her head ached, and then she brushed her hair and powdered her face and walked across to the park beside the river, opposite the hospital grounds.

When Edward Featherstone came upon her she was sitting on a fallen tree below a grassy bank, staring into the water beyond the bullrushes. He sat down beside her. "You're feeling fit?"

"I—yes, I'm all right now. Just a cut on my head. It was good of you—the roses..." she said incoherently. His nearness had already brought her to a quivering awareness, and she knew she was blushing violently. "They were lovely."

"I'm glad you liked them. I was sorry when I heard." He let his arm rest on the bough behind her, and she could feel the warmth of his hand on her shoulder-blade, although he did not touch her. "It was bad luck."

"Yes." The silence fell thickly between them and she longed to break it, but she knew that whatever she might say would sound fatuous. And then she relaxed. There was no real need to talk. He was clearly quite content to sit there at her side, saying nothing, watching the swans on the river and the paddling children on the opposite bank.

At last he murmured, "So peaceful here." Then he looked at her directly. "We'll take a boat."

He didn't say, "Would you like that?" Vivien reflected. Just "We'll take a boat." It was strangely satisfying to have a decision made for her, not to have to think. His quiet mastery swept away all her defences. She said, simply, "Yes," and got up to follow him down to the boathouse. It was almost like sleep-walking, she felt. She seemed to have no volition of her own at all. Yet she was perfectly content to obey, to follow where he led. There was no resistance, and no thought of resistance, in her mind. It was as right and as natural as the obedience of a pliable child.

He made no move to touch her again, even when they moored in the shadow of an autumn-gilded willow, hanging low over the water by the bank downstream. She trailed her fingers in the cool water, and revelled in the quietness.

Suddenly she looked up to meet his eyes, golden and compelling, and was held for long seconds by their strange light. She turned away, and to cover her confused feelings she said, "How can I lay my hands on two hundred pounds?"

"Two hundred pounds? Do you need it urgently?"

She found herself telling him about Dick's car. "He *can't* be left to pay it himself," she explained. "It's utterly unfair. I dare say he can afford it, but that's not the point."

He thought for a little while, and then he said, "You could borrow it."

"I wish I could! But I don't know anyone with that much to spare. Housemen don't save so much, and my mother couldn't spare it. And I've no friends who'd be able to, as far as I know. In any case, I couldn't *ask*. It's not the sort of thing one can."

He smiled slowly, looking into her eyes until she felt the hot colour rising again. "I will lend you two hundred pounds."

"*You* will? But that's ridiculous! I couldn't possibly allow you to. No, of course not. It—it's most awfully kind of you to offer it, but I can't possibly do that."

He waved away all she said. "You shall have it tomorrow. Say no more about it. You can repay me as and when you feel you can."

"But it would take ages! More than a year, even if I——"

"It doesn't matter. I can wait. As and when you can, I said." He reached for the sculls. "You'd like to go back now, wouldn't you? It's getting chilly."

The boat scarcely ruffled the surface of the water as they went slowly upstream in the twilight, and the drips from the oars were the only sounds. And when they moored again by the boathouse he moved along to kneel beside her on the red velvet cushions in the stern.

"Vivien ..." he said softly.

"Yes?"

"Let me——" He bent quickly to her upturned face and kissed her full on the lips, quickly and tenderly. His mouth left hers almost before she had begun to respond. Then he stood up to help her to her feet, and held the boat while she stepped on to the bank, her legs heavy with the desire he had roused in her, making her clumsy.

She turned to him as they reached the gate of the park. "I'll go on ahead. It—it's better that way."

He nodded. "Of course." They had said no more about the money, but she knew that she was going to accept it. His mastery of her will was already so complete that she knew she would do whatever he suggested. She was a stranger to herself, while she was near him, and she no longer had any insight into her own motives. He had only to touch her, she felt, and she would no longer have any volition of her own. It was a queer, satisfying feeling, and very peaceful.

*   *   *

In the morning, Rena brought her breakfast to her room on a tray. "Fine," she said. "You look lots more rested, Viv. I'm glad. You looked played out last time I saw you." She put the tray on the bedside table and sat on the edge of the bed. "And no wonder."

"I ought to be up and doing."

"Rubbish. Dick says you're to stay off for the weekend. And he's still the R.S.O. around here, as far as I know."

"Acting Casualty Officer as well," Vivien mentioned. "Poor Tommy. I hope he'll do all right."

"Yes, rough on him. On us, too—there's plenty to do! I don't know why I'm gossiping here, except that we're not doing our list until twelve."

Vivien drank some of her tea, and raised her eyebrows. "Why so late?"

"Don't ask *me*, my dear! Ask that Paulson woman. A fine flap *she's* in this morning."

"I thought she never flapped?" No, not even when I

caught her kissing Johnny, she thought. Even then she hadn't the grace to look embarrassed. If that's the kind of woman he likes, why, why, why did he ever bother about me? "I didn't think she had any emotions at all."

"Emotions? I wouldn't call it that. Just sheer ill-temper. I don't know what's upset her applecart this morning, but she's on a go-slow strike or something. Simply refused to hurry herself. I don't know why Dick doesn't go to Matron about it." She frowned. "She didn't even turn up until half an hour ago—long after nine."

"She lives out, then?"

"Apparently. A daft arrangement for a theatre sister, but I gather she's on the phone and doesn't live far away."

"I thought they couldn't, unless they were married."

Rena stood up impatiently. "They can't, officially. But she seems to have used her big eyes on Matron to some effect and got permission."

Vivien, for no reason at all, suddenly flashed back to the note she had received with Edward's roses. "Rena..." she began. "Will you tell me something?"

Rena was still looking moodily out of the window. "If I can."

"You said—you said he stuck to you out of a sense of duty. Can you tell me about it? Or——"

"You're thinking about Johnny, of course?" Vivien let her go on thinking so; there was no point in anything else. "Don't do it, Viv. Not if your feelings tell you it's wrong." She sat down again and examined her nails interestedly. "Yes, he did. And I'd learned to—to almost hate him for it. One feels so *cheap*."

"What happened, Rena?"

"He was very young, and I was only eighteen. He was just qualified. We ran away and married, and it was wonderful—at first. Then we were having a baby." She swallowed. "He—he found somebody else. She was lovely—and she was very rich. I didn't blame him. But he stayed with me because of the baby. He stayed until we came to loathe one another at times." She stood up and went over to the door. "And then I lost the baby. Viv, I tell you, I was almost glad!"

"I'm so sorry, Rena. I can't tell you."

74

"Almost glad," Rena repeated unseeingly as she stood there. "But now I'd give my whole career—everything—to have that child alive." She opened the door and looked out blankly into the corridor, and pushed back the heavy swag of yellow hair above her eyes. "It would have been a boy."

There was nothing Vivien could say.

Then Rena shrugged and pulled herself together. "Oh well, that's old hat. Sorry if I was boring you, Viv. See you later." She shut the door crisply behind her and Vivien heard her high heels clicking along the corridor and down the stairs.

So that was how it was? But she hadn't told the end of the story. Where was her husband now? What had happened in the end? She had said she was not free. . . .

At eleven o'clock Vivien was dressed and tidying her room when the housemaid came up. "A letter for you, Miss Bromwich." She held out a thick envelope. "Just came."

"Thank you, Dorothy." There was no stamp on the envelope, and she recognised the crabbed black handwriting and flushed uncomfortably. "That's all—there's no reply."

Dorothy stared. "Didn't suppose there was," she said pertly. "It's not a telegram!" She flounced off downstairs again without bothering to pick up the tray Vivien had left outside the door.

There was nothing in the envelope, when she tore it open, but forty five-pound notes. So he had kept his word. . . .

Vivien thrust it into the pocket of her cardigan and went straight over to Casualty. Dick was in the minor ops theatre, one of the nurses told her. "It's all right, Nurse," Vivien said. "I'll wait until he's free. Don't bother him now."

While she waited she watched the clinic nurses marshalling their rows of waiting patients. Not such long rows, she reflected, as in the old days before Matron had instituted the appointments system. Even so, there were still plenty of people milling about in the big hall.

Sister, passing by, indicated a grey marasmic baby, lying sprawled as vacantly as a rag doll on the lap of a slatternly, red-nailed girl on the front bench of Dr. Jameson's section. "You see what I mean?" she said. "We keep them alive, and what do they become, that kind? Morons, delinquents, layabouts, probably. We're overbalancing the lower levels of the population with our clever doctoring, aren't we?"

Vivien shook her head. She looked at the sluttish young mother and thought of Rena. "There's a powerful argument against it, Sister. Just suppose keeping that child alive is to entirely reshape its mother's life? To let it die, then, would be unforgivable."

"Reshape her life?" Sister's little laugh was no more than a bark. "It would take more than a child to reshape *her* life, Miss Bromwich! Anyone can see what *she* is!"

"But if she had to order her life to fit in with the child——"

"Ah! That would be something. Only you see, she won't. It's the child who will suffer. And then society will suffer because of the child. And so it goes on. No, you're far too much of an idealist, Miss Bromwich. You haven't seen enough of the seamy side yet."

She went on her way, smiling complacently, and Vivien wanted to hit her. If only Rena's child had lived, she thought. How different would her life have been? Would she still be as unhappy? Would the hard brightness be there quite the same?

When Dick came out of the minor ops theatre, pulling his mask down below his chin, he was surprised to see her. "What are you doing, Viv? Not thinking of working, are you? Because I'm not going to let you. Not until Monday at the earliest. See?"

"No, Dick. I—I came to see you, as soon as I could." She pushed the envelope into his hand.

"It's from Johnny and me, Dick. For the car repairs. We—we heard about the insurance trouble, and——"

He frowned. "*Johnny* heard? How?"

"Well, no, not Johnny, actually. I've not told him yet. But *I* heard. And it's what he'd want to do."

Dick shoved the envelope into her cardigan pocket. "You can think again," he said roughly. "I wouldn't think

76

of taking it, Viv. It's just one of those things. Keep it."

"You're *got* to take it, Dick! If you don't, I shall—I *shall* tell Johnny. I mean it! And then he'll tell you the same." Again she held it out. "Please take it, because I can't risk upsetting him."

Slowly Dick took it back and tapped it on his hand, thinking. Then he shrugged, and dropped his arms helplessly. "Well, if you put it that way. But I'm simply holding it until Johnny's better, you understand. And it may yet be that we shall wangle a way out of it with the insurance people. I've put my solicitor on to them." He was not happy about the money, but eventually he put it in his pocket. "You shouldn't do this, Vivien. You can't afford it."

"It's a debt of honour. I couldn't possibly rest if I didn't."

"All right. Have it your own way. But I don't like it, I tell you plainly. Now, you run off and rest, there's a dear. The world can wag on without you for a day or two."

Back in her room at the Residents' House, Vivien found the red roses standing on her dressing-table, with a scribbled note from Sister White saying: "*I thought you'd like these—they're beauties.*" She buried her face in their dark perfume and thought again of Edward, and the same old weakness ran through her body as she conjured up his eyes and his touch. I want him, she admitted to herself. I want him as I've never wanted anything. Only I don't even know who he is. But does that matter? To feel like this can't be accidental. There is some terrific purposefulness in it. . . . And then she smiled, because she was denying all her own theories of cause and effect, so hotly defended an hour or so before.

She ought, she knew, to do something about acknowledging the money. But how? Edward would be busy in the theatre, and she had no intention of entering Sister Paulson's orbit if she could help it. Certainly not on such an errand. Where did Edward live? As far as she knew, none of the porters lived in, except old Dane, down in Outpatients, who had the gate cottage.

In the end she telephoned the switchboard. "Arnold, this is Miss Bromwich. Could you tell me the address, please, of the new theatre porter?" She heard herself muttering something about the House Governor's list. "Yes, Featherstone, that's right."

"That's funny," the man said. "Oh well, I suppose it's right." She heard him riffling through his list. "It's Fifteen, The Crescent."

"Thank you, Arnold." She put the receiver down and wrote it down on the pad by the directories. "Fifteen, The Crescent," she repeated to herself. She could write him a note and drop it in there, easily.

The Crescent ran along the narrow corner of the park, across the river bridge. Edward must have been on his way home when he had met her there, she reflected. The sweep of stucco Regency houses had once been the most exclusive residential quarter of the town, but it had long ago fallen into shabby disrepute; and such houses as had not been converted into flats had been taken over as boarding-houses, whose owners did nothing to restore their flaking paint or to replace the plaster that fell from their once-beautiful shell porticoes. It seemed a great pity. But the poor little servants had so far to run from the kitchens, Vivien reminded herself. And they must have cost a fortune in fuel, to keep those high rooms heated.

Number 15 was in the middle of the curve, and it was as shabby as its neighbours. The range of different curtain colours proclaimed that it was let off in flats, or furnished rooms, and the hall, seen through open door, was bare and grimy, with no carpet on the stone stairs, and only a bare bulb to light it.

There had once been a list of names pinned up on the wall inside the porch, but the weather had washed out the ink, and those she could read were none of them Featherstone. The top flat had no name against it at all, only a scrap of paper still stuck under a rusty drawing pin, where the rest had been ripped away.

There was no sense in leaving the note in the hall, she thought, for anyone to pick up. She had better explore the building. Maybe the flats had names on their front doors.

She had no luck on the ground floor, or the first, and reluctantly climbed the narrow servants' staircase to the top. There was someone moving about in the front room

78

up there, and it was the first sign of life she had observed in the whole of the bleak, neglected building. She hesitated, and then tapped. Someone in the flat went on bumping about, apparently moving furniture across the floor, and she knocked more loudly.

"If that's you, Ted, you'll have to wait. I'm busy. Where's your key anyway?"

She waited, uncomfortably, and as she did she asked herself what it was in the husky voice that was familiar. And then at last the door was tugged open.

The girl in the black velvet housecoat had curlers in her hair, and her small feet were thrust into flat mules. But she was still, quite recognisably, Sister Paulson.

CHAPTER VI

THE kitten eyes flickered and dilated momentarily, and then Sister Paulson patted her hair apologetically and said, "Oh—Miss Bromwich. I didn't realise——" She frowned. "Were you looking for me?"

"A mistake," Vivien floundered. "They—I seem to have the wrong address." She turned blindly for the stairs. "The switchboard porter must have made a mistake."

Sister Paulson's voice was as crisp as an icicle. "I see." She folded her arms and leaned on the doorpost. "Quite a climb to no purpose!"

Hurrying down the last flight of stairs, Vivien heard the door of the top flat click shut, and her cheeks flamed. That fool of a porter! she thought bitterly. The very last person I wanted to meet.

And then she collected herself. A hospital switchboard porter rarely makes mistakes. He cannot afford to. A wrong name, a mistaken report on a patient's condition, could be serious. Vivien frowned. Then—— But there can't be any connection between them, she told herself, yet knowing, as she did so, that this was sheer wishful thinking. She thrust the note back into her pocket. She would have to leave it with the letters in the front office, she decided, and trust to luck that Edward would look in for mail. She was furious with herself for not doing just that in the first place.

She left the note on the porter's counter.

"You find him?" Arnold wanted to know.

"No, I didn't. You gave me Sister Paulson's address, Arnold. You must have made a mistake."

The man frowned and reached up to consult his list. "I thought it was funny, at the time. Mind, I didn't make this list out—it was the night chap, Wallace, did it. Sorry, Miss Bromwich. Hope you weren't inconvenienced."

"It doesn't matter. But you'd better alter the list, hadn't you?"

He nodded. "I'll see Wallace when he comes on." He looked at his watch. "Might be a nuisance if there was a general theatre call at night."

Inconvenienced, she thought. That was not quite the word. Sister Paulson's contemptuous little smile could scarcely be classed as an inconvenience. What was it about the girl that was so utterly unnerving? She was lovely to look at, and her voice and eyes were soft and feminine to the *n*th degree. But for her handshake, and her peremptory manner with her juniors, there was nothing to indicate any hardness in her at all. Yet it was impossible to feel at ease in her company. Somewhere beneath the appealing exterior there was a cold and calculating determination.

Dick Clements buttonholed Vivien after tea. "Thought you'd like to know, Viv. We'll be having Johnny up to the theatre again this evening."

"Again? But why? Not his thumb now?"

"Afraid so. We thought it might do, but it won't. We'll have to take the first joint. Tough."

"I see. Oh, well." She was at a loss for words.

"You'll come up, of course?"

She hesitated. "I—do you want me to?"

"*Want* you to? Well, no. But I thought *you'd* want to, Viv!" Dick's kind brown eyes were puzzled. "You'd rather not?"

How is he to know? she thought. He doesn't realise. . . . "Yes, thanks, Dick. I'll come up, of course. You don't

80

want me to—to assist?"

"Lord, no! Have a heart! The big shot's coming in to do it, in any case. I'll be assisting myself. About sevenish?"

"I'll be there." And so, she reminded herself, will Sister Paulson. And—and Edward.

*   *   *

Sister Paulson was indeed there when the time came. And she was certainly making her presence felt. From the surgeons' room Vivien heard her reproving first the junior, because the lotions were too cool, and then Nurse Grover, because Mr. Malcolm's instruments had not been cleaned to her liking. And lastly she flew at Edward.

Dick and Vivien looked at one another as they heard the tail-end of the onslaught. "You *fool!*" Sister Paulson was saying, as they passed the stock-room door. "How could you? You haven't the sense you were born with, have you? And you still haven't explained——"

"*Explain?*" Edward's voice was a velvety drawl. "You expect a lot, Posy!"

Vivien grimaced. "*Posy!*" she remarked. "Anything less suitable——" And she was furious with Edward.

"Her name," Dick confided, "appears to be Rosemary. But not for the kind of remembrance *I* cherish, I must admit." He smiled grimly. "Sound like a husband and wife bickering, don't they?"

"Yes," Vivien agreed automatically. And then she thought: Husband and wife! But no—that can't be the explanation. It mustn't be.

She stood in the annexe in her green "dirty" gown, talking to Mr. Malcolm as he scrubbed up. "Bad luck about Dysart's fist," he commented. "If I was quite sure it was surgery he was after, I'd be even more sorry than I am. Only I'm not."

"You're not sure, sir?" Vivien stared at him. "But he came over from medicine because he——"

Mr. Malcolm twinkled as he dried his arms on the sterile towel Nurse Grover had ready for him. "*Not* because he had a vocation for surgery, Miss Bromwich. Oh, no. But because he's the kind to try anything once. And, incidentally, because he didn't hit it off with Dr. Steinberger. I'd say he'll settle quite happily for medicine when he's recovered from the unsettling effect of all this."

Vivien was dumbfounded. "I can't believe it. If he will, of course, that solves the problem."

"He will. You'll see." Mr. Malcolm worked his gloves on carefully. "If he doesn't, my name's not Malcolm."

"Has he said so?"

"No, Miss Bromwich, he has not. He probably hasn't even thought about it yet. But he will."

"You sound very sure, sir."

"I am." He bent forward for Nurse Grover to adjust his cap. "After all," he asked simply, "what else is there for him?"

He was perfectly right, Vivien reflected. For Johnny there was no future in surgery. It was medicine or nothing.

When Bill Stedman and the junior wheeled him through from the anaesthetic room, Vivien stepped forward to help them to transfer him to the table from the trolley standing alongside, and she was involuntarily moved by his helplessness. She stood back again, against the annexe wall, because she could not bear to see Nurse Grover remove the dressing from his right hand. My fault, she was saying to herself. All my fault. And then, in spite of what Johnny had said: I can't leave him now; I can't desert him.

She sighed, and the junior looked at her, and murmured behind her mask, "What a shame, Miss Bromwich!" She felt guiltier than ever.

Mr. Malcolm worked fast and tidily, and the minor amputation was complete in a quarter of an hour. Dick looked across the table as he cut off the last suture-ends of the flap. "That should tidy it up, sir. He'll still have a certain amount of grip left."

"I think so. We managed to anchor the tendon pretty well." He turned his head. "See this, Miss Bromwich?"

Vivien forced herself to go forward and look perfunctorily at the mutilated hand. She swallowed, and nodded. "Very neat, sir. Not too much loss of function at all." But the hot tears sprang to her eyes when she thought: This is

Johnny's hand . . . and recalled its firm pressure on her back when they had danced together, and the touch of Johnny's fingers in her hair or twined in her own. That was all over. She walked blindly away into the annexe, so that Mr. Malcolm and Dick should not see the turmoil of her feelings.

Edward said softly, "Thank you for your note, Vivien."

He went on stacking the empty drums, ready to wheel them away, not looking at her at all. Yet somehow he conveyed the impression of being as acutely aware of her as she was of him.

She recovered herself at once at the sound of his voice. Johnny receded in her mind to the point where he was no longer a nagging sense of guilt. She looked at Edward's profile, the lean brown cheeks and the incredible sweeping lashes, and said, "I'm more than grateful. I can't tell you."

"You don't have to." He moved nearer to her and reached over her head for something from the shelf, and, still without looking at her directly, murmured, "To-morrow, in the park? About ten?"

There was no question in her mind as to whether she would be there or not. She simply said, "Yes."

"Evening, I mean," he added, and she nodded. It all seemed so right and inevitable, at the time.

The whole of the next day was a meaningless hiatus, something to be got through; a long, dull overture before the curtain went up. She stayed in her room for several hours, catching up on her correspondence and frankly lazing, and saw no one in the house until tea-time.

Rena joined her then, and looked at her curiously. "Where have you been hiding yourself?"

She shrugged. "Oh, writing letters, general slacking." She felt the plaster on her forehead. "I suppose I can get back to work tomorrow?"

"I should think so. If you feel fit. Do you?"

Vivien nodded. "I'm all right, Rena."

"You look a bit not-with-us, to me. But still—you should know." Rena reached out for the dish of sandwiches. "You're not eating much, are you?"

"I'm not hungry."

"Can't work without food, girl. I can't anyhow. I'm starving, after ploughing through about a million O.P.s. Dick isn't through yet."

Vivien looked up. "They haven't done anything about a new C.O. then?"

"Not yet. We're coping, between us. Had *you* thought of putting in for it?"

"*I?*" Vivien stared. "But don't be idiotic, Rena. I wouldn't stand a chance."

"I don't see why not. You've already had good surgical experience, and you're a red-hot diagnostician, from what Dr. Palmer tells me. After all, let's face it, the C.O.'s job here is pretty junior compared with the R.S.O.'s and the R.M.O.'s. And it *is* only a question of a *temporary* appointment. They've had first-rate news of Tommy—he's making great strides. He's out of the lung—back into a cuirass already. That's pretty terrific if he was a developed bulbar, isn't it?"

"But, Rena—I've never done a registrar's job even, yet!"

"This would be roughly the equivalent. And you haven't a chance of a surgical registrarship for at least another year, even with Mr. Malcolm to pull strings for you. You have to fill in somehow, and get more experience. So why not?"

"You really think I'm capable, Rena?"

"Tush, girl! Of course you are. We have all to be *capable* of doing the next job up. The only query is, will they *let* us?"

"You—you think I ought to approach the H.G. about it?"

"Let Dick do that for you. I think it was his idea, to be frank. At least, he said he had his eye on a temporary C.O., and he was certainly looking at you when he said it."

"I never knew he had so much confidence in me!"

"Diffident, that's you, Vivien! I'll tell him you're not exactly unwilling, shall I?"

Vivien nodded. "All right. If you think so." She stood up.

"You going up to see Johnny?"

Johnny was not even on the fringe of her mind, but she said, "I suppose I could. Yes."

Rena cooked one eyebrow quizzically. "You don't sound

awfully eager!"

"No. There's just nothing I can say or do to undo the damage, or to make things any better than they are; and I don't think he much wants to see me, Rena."

"You go," Rena cut in. "Damn it, you can't *not* go." She frowned. "How would *you* feel in his place?"

"I wouldn't want to see me again. And that's how he does feel, don't you see? He said so."

"I don't believe it!" Rena sounded quite uncompromising. "I simply don't believe it. The last thing Johnny would do is to blame you, or to cry off on account of what's happened."

Vivien shook her head. "Oh, no. Not on account of what's happened—the accident, I mean. It was before that. . . ."

"What was?"

"I mean—after the accident he said he'd been about to tell me that we were all washed up, and he hadn't a chance to say so before the crash." She flushed uncomfortably. "He said—he said he had found someone else."

Rena's handsome eyes blazed. "Of all the fat-heads! And you couldn't see through that little manoeuvre? How old are you?"

"It wasn't any manoeuvre—he meant it."

"Did he really? Do you really think that anything he said right then could be taken in that way? Don't you honestly think he was simply being—being noble, as they say?" She pushed back her chair impatiently. "I thought you had more intelligence, Viv, I did really. Of *course* he 'offers you your freedom', as it were. He doesn't want to put you in the position of being tied to him."

"He found someone else," Vivien told her obstinately. "He doesn't go in for that kind of dramatics. And besides . . ." She thought of the unbearable spell of Edward's physical presence, and looked at her watch. Three more hours, she thought, and I shall be alone with him.

"And besides, you're just a selfish little beast!" Rena flashed. "God knows I don't think you should stick, just because of this—this disaster, if you don't care. But you might at least *visit* the boy!"

She marched out without saying any more.

Sister Jones nodded grimly at her at the door of Ward

10. "Come to see Mr. Dysart, I suppose, Miss Bromwich? Very depressed, he's been, I'm sorry to say. Just what he needs, a nice cheerful visitor." She leaned nearer to Vivien. "There's been a solicitor to see him, and it's worried him a bit, I think. Something about the damage to the car."

"A solicitor? Was it Mr. Clements' solicitor, do you know, Sister?"

Sister Jones's dark face was screwed up as she tried to remember. "Well, that I can't say. But he did mention Mr. Clements' name, that I do know."

Vivien sighed. "Then Mr. Dysart knows that—that the insurance people don't want to pay up."

"They don't? There's a dreadful thing for you! They say the car was badly smashed. Will poor Mr. Dysart have to find the money, then, is that it?" Sister Jones tutted with concern.

"Something like that. Mr. Clements was anxious he shouldn't find out just yet."

"Then that explains it. So worried he's been looking ever since that man was here. I'd not have let him in if I'd known how it would be. We don't want Mr. Dysart upset yet, do we? It's all been a nasty shock." She stood back to let Vivien go down the corridor to Johnny's side ward. "Well, you must do what you can to cheer him up, Miss Bromwich."

Johnny lay brooding at the ceiling, and only managed a tight little smile when he saw Vivien. She said, "I hear you've had a visitor?"

"That's right. We're in a mess, Viv. Seems the insurance people aren't inclined to play ball."

"It's all right, Johnny," she said impulsively. "I've seen Dick, and it's all fixed up."

"You mean they've changed their minds?" He leaned on his good elbow and the lines round his mouth began to relax. "Really?"

She nodded. "I imagine so. He—he just said it was all lined up. So I suppose that's the end of it. You needn't worry any more about it." She sat down beside the bed. "How do you feel?"

"Still not too clever, Viv." He lay back again. "But if

86

you really mean it—if they've really got this thing worked out—I feel a mile better!"

"Good. I'm glad." There seemed nothing more to say. She thought, I can't say anything, yet, about the future. Maybe he hasn't faced up to it yet, that he won't be able to go on with surgery. For want of something safe to say she began: "Rena seems to think I'd make a temporary Casualty Officer. I don't know whether——?"

"*You* would?" The cloud came down again, and Johnny turned his face away from her. "I see." He sounded resigned.

"I know she's talking through her hat," Vivien told him hurriedly. "I shan't apply, of course."

Johnny shrugged. "Don't let me stand in your way."

"*You?* Were you thinking of it for yourself?" *Now* what had she said?

"It doesn't matter."

"Oh, but Johnny—I never thought! I thought you'd ——"

"You thought!" he told her bitterly. "You thought I'd give up, just like that!" He snapped his fingers. "Is that it?"

She swallowed. "No, you know I don't think that. Not that—well, not that you could be blamed if you did."

"Thanks," he said curtly. And then his voice went up a couple of tones. "I don't want any allowances made for me, thank you. 'Poor old Dysart.' I suppose that's what they're saying, is it? 'Poor old Dysart, he'll have to go back to the medical side.' That's the talk in the house, is it?"

She lowered her own voice with an effort. "You *know* we're not saying those things, Johnny. As for me, I'm just saying, 'My fault, my fault, my fault'—that's all." She stopped, her lips trembling.

Johnny closed his eyes. "It—was—not—your—fault," he said slowly and distinctly. "Not. Got it?" He flapped his good hand irritably. "Now go, Viv. You're doing no good here."

"Very well. I'll go." She hesitated at the foot of the bed. "Johnny . . ."

"Goodnight, Viv."

"Goodnight, then." She groped at the cold bed-rail. "And good-bye. I'd better not come again, if that's how you feel, had I?"

He murmured that she could please herself, and turned his face away from her, tight-mouthed.

Sister Jones darted out of the linen-room as she passed. "Cheered him up, have you, Miss Bromwich?" She looked searchingly at Vivien's face, and her black button eyes saw all there was to see. She sighed. "No? There now! I did hope it'd do him good to see you. Still worried, is he?" Vivien shrugged. "Not about the insurance. Just about his job, I think. Mr. Malcolm thought—we all thought—that he might come round to the idea of going back to medicine. But it won't be as simple as that."

"Nothing worth while ever *is* simple, Miss Bromwich. It's not to be expected that he'll come round just yet. Give him a few days. You'll come and see him tomorrow, will you?"

"I don't know. One of us will be in, of course. Goodnight, Sister."

She could feel Sister Jones's dark gaze on her shoulder-blades all the way to the lift. I've upset him, she thought miserably. And she knows it. She'll go in to him now and try to find out what we've said to one another. And Johnny will bite her head off if she does.

In the hall Mr. Malcolm, in his overcoat, was pacing up and down beside the porter's office. She turned away from the side door and hurried to meet him. "Good evening sir, I'm sorry, I had no idea you were in. They——"

"That's all right. Purely a social call, Miss Bromwich. I just wanted a word—— Ah, here she is!" He smiled up at Rena, running down the stairs, and Rena beamed back.

"Good evening, sir."

"Evening, my dear. Are you still on duty? Or can you spare a——"

Vivien left them talking, Rena looking down from the bottom step, one long hand on the newel post, and Mr. Malcolm smiling up at her in a way that would have astonished Sister Blount. It would astonish Bill Stedman too, she realised, when she saw him coming towards her along the bottom corridor.

She waylaid him, trying to think up an excuse that he would swallow. "Oh, Bill—are you busy?"

"What is it, Vivien?" He halted, looking at her seriously. "Anything wrong?"

"No. No, nothing wrong. You remember that chorea girl we sent over from our side?"

He tipped his head back, remembering. "Yes, I remember. The one you had in O.P."

"Could you let me know her blood group, some time? For some statistics I'm keeping. I don't know whether we ever grouped her: we should have done, but if we did I've forgotten, and I haven't her notes any more."

"Of course. Want me to check now?"

"No, no hurry. Only if I didn't ask you now, while I think of it, I should forget, and then I'd have to disinter her papers from the files. You know what a game that is."

"I won't forget, Viv. That all?"

He stood there swinging his stethoscope, obviously waiting for her to dismiss him. Surely Rena would have finished talking to Mr. Malcolm by the time he reached the hall, she thought. And there was no more excuse to delay him. She nodded. "That's all. Thanks, Bill."

Instead of hurrying away, he walked to the side door with her, and before he turned back to the main corridor he said, "How's Johnny?" He reached across her for the door handle. "Seen him this evening?"

"He's pretty low, I'm afraid."

"I see. Well, who wouldn't be? But he'll bob up. He's too big a chap to whine for long. You know Johnny."

She smiled uneasily. "Yes, I know Johnny. Thanks, Bill. See you later."

Do I know Johnny? She wondered. Do I even know myself? It seemed such a short time since everything had been sane and happy, and there had been nothing in the world to worry about. And now—— She lifted her head and quickened her step as she set off up the road. It was a waste of time to think in circles about something that couldn't be helped. She and Johnny no longer concerned one another. And she had made her choice: she would put all her working energies into making a success of her job for Mr. Malcolm. It was all cut and dried.

But as she let herself into the quiet hall of the Residents' House she thought, Cut and dried? But is it? And then, involuntarily, so violently that she almost spoke aloud, she reminded herself: Edward, Edward. What about Edward? Where will he fit in?

Half-way up the stairs she met Dick Clements coming down. She stopped. "Dick, I'm glad I've seen you. . . . Look, I've been a perfect idiot. . . ."

"Surely not?" He smiled down at her, easily. "All right. Tell me, then."

"Well, I—I suppose Rena was really only theorising, but she said she had an idea you'd thought, perhaps, of giving me a chance in Casualty. And I said as much to Johnny. He simply blew his top. So——"

Dick was shaking his head at her. "Rena was surmising, Viv." He put one finger on her arm. "Hold it! I'm not saying that I didn't have you in mind at one point; or that you're not capable. I'm saying that I haven't mentioned your name—or anyone else's for that matter—in this connection as yet. And now I most certainly wouldn't."

She frowned. "Oh? Then you're fixed up? Or do you mean——?"

"No. Just because I know that Johnny's mind is working in that direction."

"But he couldn't do the job, Dick! Not with *his* hands."

"We don't know yet, Viv. He couldn't do any major surgery. Obviously. Maybe he won't be able to do minor ops. I grant you that. But with a really good H.S. he could hold the fort down there until Cartwright's well again."

"I see." She flushed, and looked at him awkwardly, up the two steps that divided them. "Well, that's fine. I'm sure that's just what he wants. What he needs."

Dick smiled. "With a good H.S., I said, Viv. The good H.S. being you. Or I had you in mind. How do you feel about a change round?"

"*Me?* Oh, no! It wouldn't work, Dick. Honestly."

"No? Oh, well. It was just an idle thought. I don't expect your chief would have fussed unduly. He can't use a new registrar just yet."

She shook her head again. "*Johnny* wouldn't want it,

Dick. It's Johnny I'm thinking of. Not me. It—it would be disastrous."

"All right." He patted her arm again and stood aside for her to pass. "Don't give it another thought. We'll cope somehow." He looked disappointed, but his voice was as casual and friendly as ever.

She stared after him. He means so well, she told herself. But for me to work with Johnny—for me, a woman, to be the one to act as his crutch and do the things he'll have to cry off doing! Could anything be less diplomatic, the way things are?

Rena joined her at supper, looking oddly thoughtful. "Hallo , Viv." She sat down opposite and reached for the salad dish. "Not out, then?"

"No. I thought *you* were." She pushed the mayonnaise across the table. "I'd have waited if I'd——"

"Why on earth would *I* be out? I'm not much of a gadder, you know that. Is this the freshest bread Winnie can dig out?"

Vivien eyed her uncertainly, half afraid to probe. "I thought maybe you'd gone somewhere with my boss."

Rena looked down at her coffee cup, and stirred it hard. "No. Good lord, no. He just called in to——" She looked up at Bill Stedman in the doorway. "Just to borrow a book of mine." Her voice trailed off, and then she smiled at Bill. "What's on *your* mind?"

He pulled up a chair, and Vivien filled his cup and passed it to him. "Nothing, really. I was just concentrating on remembering to tell Vivien the chorea girl's blood group. She's O, anyway, Viv."

"Thanks, Bill. Nice of you to remember." She got up and pushed her chair under the table. "I'll leave you two to entertain one another."

"Going out after all?" Rena glanced up at her. "You look as though a spot of fresh air might be a sound idea, I admit."

Up in her room she was suddenly aware that her hands were shaking as she reached down a soft green jersey dress from her wardrobe. Johnny had never liked it. He had wrinkled his nose and said, "It's not *you*, Viv. It makes you look—dangerous. I can't think why." And

91

she had never worn it since. It was the colour, she supposed. He always hated green.

She *felt* dangerous, she admitted. The conflicts of the day had built up into a close, restricting fence that she longed to crash through headlong. She felt instinctively that Edward would understand; that some current flowing between them would draw off the tension she felt.

She took a good deal of trouble in making up her face. Far more trouble, she realised, than she had ever taken for Johnny. But then Johnny was simple and unsophisticated, and he liked her to be the same, and she had been.

She frowned at the mirror, and deliberately went over her lips again, deepening the colour. That was all over. Johnny was over. She was no longer the same person. There wasn't a reason in the world, now, why she should repress the excitement that was making her fingers so unsteady.

Ten o'clock, Edward had said. She slipped across the road in the shadow of the buildings, and through the never-locked kissing gate at the corner of the park, to walk quickly along the chrysanthemum-spiced path to the water's edge.

He will be waiting by the fallen tree, she thought. And when he hears me he will stand up and come towards me, and I shall run. . . .

But there was nobody there. The only sound, as she sat down on the tree-trunk, hugging her knees, was the faint lapping of water at the gate of the boat-shed, and the rustling of tiny creatures in the grass on the bank.

She sat there for nearly an hour before, cramped and chilled, she got to her feet and began, slowly, to make her was back to the gate. And then he came running. He stood in front of her, with a dark felt hat pulled down over his eyes so that he looked a different person until he pulled it off. "Vivien, I'm sorry. It's a miracle you're still here. I didn't think you would be."

Because her excitement and her need of him had died a bitter little death while she waited, her temper flashed out unexpectedly. "You didn't think! No, don't touch me." She fended off his reaching hands. "I'm going."

He stood perfectly still and his arms dropped to his sides. He didn't say anything at all. Out of sheer perversity she flung herself at him then. "Edward, Edward! I'm sorry." She reached up on tiptoe, brushing his chin with her lips. "Forgive me."

He kissed her. His mouth came down hard on hers, bruising her lips so that she almost cried out. Not with the pain, but with the release it afforded her. Hurt me, hurt me, she was saying mentally. Hurt me, Edward, and set me free.

It was all a headlong confusion for the next few minutes. His lips and hands were everywhere, it seemed. But then he took her by the shoulders and shook her gently, and bent his head to look at her closely. His eyes flickered gold in the moonlight reflected from the dark water.

"Vivien, I'm going away."

She stiffened. "Away? But where? *Why*, Edward?"

He kissed her hair, and let her go again. "It's best." He was evading her eyes now. "It's best, Vivien."

"For whom? Edward, where are you going?" She tugged at the lapels of his coat like a child anxious for attention. "Where?"

He stroked the nape of her neck, as he had done when she had let him soothe her migraine. "I don't know yet. North, I think. But you see—this can't go on."

She burst into a wild spasm of crying, clinging to him and beating her head on his chest. "Don't leave me. You can't."

"I must." He put her away from him again, and suddenly his voice was hard and clear. "Don't for God's sake make so much *fuss*, Vivien. You're not making it easy for me."

"*Easy?* For *you?* What about me?" She was shivering. And then she realised he was saying something about "the money". She stared at him stupidly. "The money?"

"Yes. The two hundred. I'm sorry, Vivien. I shall *have* to have it back. I need it."

She could scarcely believe that she had heard him correctly. "You—you want it *back?*" It was incredible.

He nodded impatiently. "That's what I said. You must post it to me, Vivien. Poste Restante, Manchester."

"But I *can't!* I haven't got it. And I can't ask——"

His grip on her shoulders tightened. He was hurting her, she thought dully. "You'll have to get it somehow, Vivien. And you mustn't tell anyone where you're sending it. Do you hear?" He put his hat on and looked at her again. "I'm going now. I have a lift organised."

He turned abruptly and left her standing there, dazedly listening to his footsteps fading away in the distance.

Too late, panic rose in her. I can't get it back! she thought. What am I to do? What have I done? She ran, stumbling, to the gate, and looked up and down the road for him. He had gone, and there was nobody about but a policeman, walking in the opposite direction. And over the road, in the Residents' House, the lights glowed yellow from Rena's room and Bill's. She hurried towards them, reaching out instinctively towards the normal and the known as a refuge from her anxiety.

CHAPTER VII

VIVIEN raced up the stairs of the Residents' House, her pulse still hammering, and paused outside Rena's door to collect herself, pushing back her ruffled hair and smoothing her crumpled collar. In the momentary silence she heard Rena laughing softly—and the laugh ended on a sob.

She tapped the door lightly and walked straight in. There was no time to back out before Bill Stedman swung round to face her, murmured something, and pushed clumsily past her into the corridor. Rena went on sitting on the edge of her bed, with her face in her hands, and didn't look up.

Vivien went over and touched her shoulder. "I'm sorry. I didn't mean to butt in, Rena. Anything I can do?"

Rena shook her head slowly, and finally dried her eyes and looked across ruefully at the dressing-table mirror. "Not a thing. Just making an ass of myself, that's all."

"Not like you." Vivien sat down. "Bill been upsetting you?"

"On the contrary. I've been upsetting him. I wish——" She stopped, and blew her nose hard. "What's your trouble, anyhow?"

"Mine?" Vivien blinked. "Oh, nothing you can help. Just my own idiocy."

Rena began to powder her face. "You better tell me," she said. "It's been obvious for days that you're completely disorganised. There are times, you know, when the gay laugh isn't the answer. It isn't just Johnny you're bothered about, is it?"

I can't tell her, Vivien thought. I can't tell anyone. And then, incredibly, she found herself pouring out the whole stupid story.

When she had finished Rena sat very still, drawing deeply on her cigarette, staring into the mirror. Then she said gently, "You're in a bit of a spot, aren't you, Viv? What are you going to do?"

"What *can* I do?"

Rena shrugged. "It rather depends on how you feel about—Featherstone." She held up her hand. "No! Don't tell me. I know. The symptoms are the same whether it's real or not. You're the only one who can sort it out. The only one who knows, deep down, whether it's worth having." She stood up, and began to tidy her hair. "Oh, I know how it *feels,* Viv! I know only too well. But the question is, is it just—just sex? Or is there any *respect* mixed up with it?"

"Respect?" Vivien echoed. "Respect? . . . Rena, I don't know." She frowned, picturing Edward's great golden eyes, feeling his warm breath, and remembering her defenceless-ness against his kisses. She closed her eyes. "I don't know."

"Then it's just sex," Rena told her briskly. She slapped down her hairbrush and turned round. "That makes it all so much easier. Then the first thing to do is stop worrying about his confounded money. Let him whistle for it. He *told* you there was no hurry, didn't he?"

"Yes, but——"

"Well then, there's no hurry. Now, ask yourself *why* he's suddenly haring off to Manchester. It doesn't add up. Why

95

the sudden urgency? Didn't he say?"

"He—he just said something about it being best. That we couldn't go on like this. That's all."

"Oh, rubbish, Viv! Whoever heard of a man caring whether an affair 'ought' to go on or not—until it's as good as over anyhow? It's we women who do the worrying, Viv; we're the ones who ask ourselves whether it's right, and whether it's fair, and all the rest of it. Most men take as much of a woman as they can get. The nice ones are grateful, the others aren't, that's the only difference. All the big renunciation scenes are staged by women, my dear."

Her voice was suddenly hard. Vivien suddenly understood. "You mean—you mean you've just been staging one with Bill?"

"Something like that."

"But Rena—*why?* Because of Mr. Malcolm?"

Rena laughed, and lit another cigarette. Her hand trembled as she lit it. "No. Because of me."

"I see. I thought you were fond of him, but——" Vivien swallowed. "I suppose he bores you really, and you're nice to him because he's shy?"

"*Nice* to him? Ye gods! Is *that* how it looks?" She laughed shortly. "Bill's—— Well, Bill's the one. Just the one. If there could *be* one. Only it doesn't work out that way."

"But why not? Rena, *why* can't it work out that way?"

Rena looked up again, and her beautiful eyes were as empty as Bill's had been when he stumbled out into the corridor. "Why? It's simple. Because if I marry I shall want children. And there can't be any. That's all."

Vivien stared. "You—you're quite sure about that, I suppose?"

"Quite. It—it just wouldn't be fair to any man to marry him on those terms. Would it?"

"A man who loved you would have to accept it, surely? Have you told Bill?"

"Of course not! You know Bill. He'd have said just that, that it made no odds, that it was *me* he wanted. Wouldn't he? And then, later, he'd have regretted marrying some one who couldn't give him children. No, Viv. I didn't give him the chance to be noble about it."

Vivien was suddenly angry. "So you'd rather hurt him instead? By telling him you don't care for him? How *could* you, Rena?"

"I don't know." Rena went over to the door. "I don't *know* how. But somehow I managed it. Let's leave it at that. Coming down to see if Winnie will make some coffee?"

Now that Rena had herself in hand again, all Vivien's own anxiety flooded back. She shivered. "Coffee? Yes, I suppose it's a good idea. I'm cold."

"Of course you are." Rena flung an arm across her shoulders. "Poor old Viv! Look, if you're really desperate, *I'll* help over the money. But only if you're desperate. So don't fret. I *could* raise it, if it meant saving you from prison or something as urgent as that. But I don't propose to just to suit Featherstone. See?" She gripped Vivien's shoulder, and then let her go on ahead down the stairs.

When Winnie had gone off, grumbling, to make the coffee, the common-room telephone rang and Vivien reached out for it. It was Dick Clements. "That you, Vivien?" he asked. "Rena there?"

"Yes, Dick."

"Is she fit for any more work tonight?"

Vivien looked across at Rena, lighting yet another cigarette with a spill from the fire. She was pale still, and her hand shook a little. "No," she told him firmly. "I don't think so. Why?"

Dick hesitated. "It's—Mr. Malcolm. Just landed in Cas with a head injury."

"Brought it in himself, d'you mean?" She frowned. "Is it a P.P., or something?"

"No. You're not with me. He has the head injury. We'll have to have him in the theatre right away. Maybe it'd be better if you *didn't* tell Rena. I mean, they're pretty pally, and——"

"I wasn't going to," she reassured him. "I'll come down now." She put the telephone down and looked across at Rena again as she went to the door. "Keep the coffee hot for me," she mentioned. "Dick wants me in Cas for a bit."

Rena turned round. "Oh, but—— No, *I'll* go, Viv."
She stubbed out her cigarette at once. "You stay here."

"Sorry, I'm the one he asked for," Vivien smiled. "Shan't
be long, I expect." She got out while Rena was still staring
at her, and hurried down to Casualty.

There was a policeman outside the first cubicle, and
inside Dick Clements and Barber, the Casualty night
nurse, were frowning at one another across Mr. Malcolm,
lying on the couch grey-faced.

Dick nodded. "Nice of you, Viv. Look at this." He
lifted the wad of gauze from Mr. Malcolm's temple, and
showed her the deep wound. "Have to do a decompression,
etcetera, etcetera. And fast. You all right to assist? There
isn't time to get one of the big boys in to do it, or I would.
I don't want the responsibility?"

She nodded. "Have you called the theatre?"

"I have, Miss Bromwich," Nurse Barber murmured.
"They should be ready by now. Shall I prep his head here,
or will you do it up there?"

"We'll do it up there, Nurse." Dick stood back from
the couch. "Send him up in ten minutes, will you?"

*   *   *

In the lift Vivien looked up at Dick. "How did it
happen?"

"That's what the cop wants to know! The old boy was
coshed or something, by all accounts."

"But what on earth *for*?" The idea of anyone wanting
to attack Mr. Malcolm seemed ludicrous.

"Robbery with violence, I imagine. He has a prosperous
look about him, and there are plenty of not-nice types in
this neighbourhood."

"Where did they find him? And was there anything
missing?"

"Shouldn't think so. He was all buttoned up, nice and
tidy. Not far away, actually. The cop heard a kerfuffle
going on outside the main entrance—the consultants' car
park was closed, and there was a stack of cars outside.
And he found the old boy spark out against his own wheel.

Maybe he disturbed a car thief, or something. Anyhow, he's been slugged pretty hard."

The theatre corridor was still in darkness when they left the lift, and only the light in the duty room was showing. Dick frowned. "That woman!" he grumbled. "Ought to have got things moving by now. Where the devil is she?"

Sister Paulson must have been coming up the stairs beside the lift, because she appeared out of the dusk behind Dick as silently as a cat. "If you mean me, I'm here, R.S.O. I came as soon as I was called." She looked at Vivien sidelong, and her eyes were cool slits between their lashes. "Are we in a hurry?"

"*We* are, Sister," Vivien told her. "The patient is Mr. Malcolm himself. A head injury. Mr. Clements wants to decompress. As quickly as possible, please."

Sister Paulson swept into the duty room, and they heard her voice raised in there. Dick smiled grimly. "Poor Grover," he murmured. Sounds as though he's getting it." He held open the door of the surgeon's room for Vivien, and followed her in. "Doesn't even seem to be any porter on duty."

So it was Featherstone's evening on call? And he had gone. Or had he? Had it all been an idiotic hallucination? Would he suddenly come through the door of the annexe, drums in each hand, and his eyes as gentle as ever? Vivien searched for her boots, and thought confusedly.

But by the time the theatre was ready, and the trolley was in the ante-room, there was still only Nurse Grover to do all the running about. Dick pulled up his gloves and looked across the empty table at Sister Paulson. "Are you quite ready? Have you no more staff? No porter?"

Her eyes blazed over her mask. "No, Mr. Clements. And don't ask me why. I don't know. What's more, I don't care. I should have thought there were quite enough of us to deal with a minor op." She stood at her table concentrating on her suture needles, but it was clear that she *did* care, very much, Vivien decided. In fact, Sister Paulson was very angry indeed, and all the usual honey was gone from her voice. "Would you like to begin now?"

Nurse Grover and the Casualty nurse got Mr. Malcolm

on to the table and Vivien took the mops from Sister Paulson and began cleaning up at once, before she clipped fresh sterile towels round the ugly wound. Then she stood back while Dick made a neat incision, and reached for the trephine. Its grating whir sickened her a little, as usual, and she was glad when he nodded and laid it back on the trolley behind him. It took him nearly half an hour to tidy the job up, but by the time he had finished and was stitching, Mr. Malcolm's colour was already improving.

"He'll do now," Dick said. "We'd better get him on to a glucose and saline drip right away, I think. Where are we putting him—Ward Ten side ward, I suppose?"

Nurse Grover cleared her throat. "The nurse from Ward Ten is here for him now, Mr. Clements. Is she to bring the trolley in?"

"Yes, she can take him down. Tell them to get him up on small blocks and Miss Bromwich and I will be right down, if they'll set for an intravenous saline. Who's on duty down there?"

"Nurse said Sister Jones was still on."

Dick grunted. "Doesn't that woman ever go off duty? All right, Nurse. Carry on. We shan't be more than a few minutes." He reached up to untie his mask, and pulled off his cap. "Thanks, Vivien. That was quite a nasty crack, wasn't it? Wonder who the chap was?"

"Could have been anyone. I mean, the car parks are right on the main road. It didn't have to be anyone from here, did it?" She felt her voice rising, and only then realised what was in her mind. Dick was looking at her oddly as he stripped off his gloves. "Not that I thought it was, of course," she added hurriedly.

"I should bally well think not! Who on earth would? Why, he's one of the best-liked chaps on the list! Nobody from here would *dare*."

Vivien went ahead of him into the surgeons' room after she had washed, and retrieved her white jacket. She must have been mad, she thought, to have let such a fantastic idea enter her head. As she stood there combing her hair before going down to the wards, Sister Paulson flung the door open. "If you're going to Ward Ten, Miss Bromwich, you might ask Sister to kindly send up a nurse for Harkness's clothes." She dumped a loose parcel on the table. "I haven't staff to run all over the hospital. The ward nurse should have taken them down this afternoon. Slackness!"

Vivien frowned. Who on earth was Harkness? And what were his clothes doing in the theatre block? "A patient's clothes?" She put her comb away and turned back from the mirror. "I can take them down with me, if that's all. But why are they here?"

"The man was brought straight up here from Casualty, Miss Bromwich. I've never known such a practice in any hospital I've ever worked in. And so——"

"I suppose it was an emergency." Vivien sighed. "Of course it isn't usual, but I suppose there *are* times when——"

Sister Paulson had already flounced out. The duty room door banged behind her.

She left the parcel in Sister Jones's linen-room as she passed the door, and joined Dick in the side ward. He already had the drip fixed, and was holding up the foot of the bed while Nurse Colman adjusted the wooden blocks. Mr. Malcolm's lips were moving. "That...fellow..." he murmured.

Vivien bent over him, feeling his pulse. "You'll be all right now, Mr. Malcolm. We've taken care of your head, sir. Just a bump." As his eyes flickered for a moment she was impelled to say, "*What* fellow? Who was it, sir?"

But he couldn't tell her. "That fellow...what'sisname ...?" He gave up and closed his eyes again. "Don't know."

Dick came up beside her. "Don't worry him now. He'll tell us later. Time enough to bother him when I have to let the police in. I've stalled them for the time being; said he was unconscious."

Sister Jones came up quietly from the shadows beyond the circle of light round the bed. She checked the drip, straightened the blankets, and smiled. "He'll do now, Mr. Clements. I think I'll go off duty. Unless you want me for anything?"

"No, thank you, Sister." Dick shook his head at her. "You should have gone long ago. A glutton for it, aren't you?"

"You surely didn't think I should go off duty when I knew our Mr. Malcolm was coming up, did you, Mr. Clements? A fine thing!" She unpinned the little bunch of keys from her apron bib, and slipped her cuffs on.

Vivien held up one finger. "Oh, Sister! I've dumped a parcel in the linen-room—clothes for Harkness, whoever he may be. They were in the theatre."

"*You* brought them down, Miss Bromwich? What next! Thank you very much, but Sister should have sent a nurse down with them. Thank you."

Dick laughed when she had bustled out. "Sister Jones has a great sense of the proper," he murmured. "Evidently it isn't done for house surgeons to carry parcels! Remind me to lay on a porter next time you have any luggage, Viv." Now that Mr. Malcolm was out of danger he was relieved, Vivien thought. She had shaken off his concern like a loose coat. She wished she could do the same with her own—but it was not so simple.

Rena would know what to do, she told herself. By now Rena would have thought it all out. She remembered that she still had to tell Rena about Mr. Malcolm. But back in the Residents' House she found Rena's light out, and there was no answer to her knock. Only Dick seemed to be about, and he was the last person she could tell.

*   *   *

She was in her dressing-gown, trying to read, when the tap came on her door. Night Sister stood outside, as quiet as a ghost in the dark corridor. She came round the door apologetically. "I'm sorry to come and bother you at this hour, Miss Bromwich. But maybe you can help me to clear something up. It's rather difficult."

"Mr. Malcolm's all right, isn't he?" Vivien pulled a chair forward. "Do sit down, Sister. You don't get many chances."

"No, I won't. I'd never get up again, Miss Bromwich, it isn't Mr. Malcolm. He's—well, so-so. Not too bad. It's this man Harkness. You haven't seen him, have you, yet?"

Harkness. The name sounded familiar. "No, I haven't. What is he?"

"An amputation from the knee. He was admitted this afternoon. It seems he was taken straight to the theatre, and——"

She remembered then. "Oh, of course. I took his clothes down. What's wrong? He's not bleeding?"

Sister's pale face moved to and fro. "No. There's nothing wrong with him. But you say you took his clothes down.... That's what I wanted to ask you. Who gave them to you, Miss Bromwich?"

"Why, Sister Paulson. She brought them out of the duty room, and——"

"I see. And were they wrapped up?"

"They had a piece of brown paper rolled round them, yes. I can't say it was a proper parcel. Why?"

"It's all very difficult." Sister sighed and looked down at her apron bib, making her chin double. "It seems that Sister Paulson can't have any notion of the way we deal with patients' belongings. She left everything in the man's pockets, instead of listing it and getting a receipt.... And it appears that there's a great deal of money missing."

"Oh, *no*! Does Matron know yet?"

"She does not! I'm doing all I can to work this out before I report it, Miss Bromwich. Can you help me in any way?"

"Well, no. No, I can't, Sister. All I know is that Sister Paulson gave me the parcel—at least, she left it on the table in the surgeons' room—and I took it down to the ward and left it in the linen-room. Sister Jones wasn't there, but I told her a few minutes later. And I presume she took it from there." She frowned. "How much money? Does the man himself know?"

"How else would *we* know? Of course he knows. Nurse made a list and took it to him to sign, so that she could give him a receipt, and he said at once, 'My money's gone. My wallet.' Mind, I soothed him; I said that someone would have taken charge of it for him. But I can't keep him quiet very long unless I produce his money."

"Have you asked Sister Paulson about it, Sister?"

Sister nodded. "Naturally. Her story is similar to yours. That the man's clothes had been packed up, and she merely handed them to you."

Vivien sank down on the edge of her bed and stared up. "Packed up by *whom*?"

"There was two hundred odd pounds," Sister added. "Seems the man Harkness is a second-hand car dealer—they usually carry large amounts in cash, he tells me. It seems a rather tricky trade—cheques aren't the thing. As to who packed them up, Sister didn't seem to know. One of the theatre staff, I suppose."

"Then . . ." Vivien's lips were suddenly cold. "Then we'd better find out, hadn't we?"

"Not 'we', Miss Bromwich. It's not really your affair. I merely came to check with you, in case you could throw any light. But obviously you can't."

"No, I can't. I can only tell you that *I* passed on the parcel just as I got it."

Sister's pale eyebrows went up towards her spruce cap. "I didn't imagine anything else, Miss Bromwich. Well, I'll have to ask you to keep it to yourself until morning. I may be able to clear it all up quietly. I shall try." She opened the door. "Thank you. I'm sorry to have bothered you. Goodnight, Miss Bromwich." Vivien watched her sail down the corridor and turn the corner for the stairs. Then she raced after her.

"Sister!"

Half-way down, Night Sister looked back and stood still. "Yes?"

"Did you—did you *tell* Sister Paulson why you were enquiring?"

"I didn't tell her what was missing, no. I said his things didn't seem to be all there, and did she know whether they were all in the parcel."

"Then don't. And then if she *knows* what's missing——Don't you see?"

Sister turned away. "You are uncharitable, Miss Bromwich! But I take your point. Goodnight."

Vivien went back to her room then, but it was a long time before she managed to get to sleep. And just as she was on the verge of dozing she found herself thinking of

Johnny. What *would* he do? Would he really persist in trying to do the Casualty job, in spite of his hand? She would go and see him again in the morning. Maybe he would be more cheerful. Although the spark between them had died so miserably, she might still be of some use to him. If he needed her.... But he had shown clearly that he didn't. Very clearly, whatever Rena might say.

She thought sleepily of Rena and Bill Stedman. It was a great temptation to intervene in other people's affairs. Surely, if Bill *knew* how Rena felt...He ought to know, Vivien told herself, as she drifted into sleep. It wasn't fair. If it had been Johnny...But Rena was Rena, and she would never forgive anyone's intrusion. It was a wonder she had confided as much as she had. Tomorrow she might be regretting it.

* * *

She and Dick were first down to breakfast. He stared at her, and she told him defiantly, "I'm working today. All day. Whether you like it or not."

"Oh? You are? Very well, if that's the way you feel. And you might shove the sugar over." He reached for the bowl. "Why the energy?"

"It isn't energy. It's restlessness, I suppose. And you'll be busy too, with no Mr. Malcolm to call on, I dare say."

"I dare say I will. Look, Viv—you don't have to——?"

"I do." Irritation suddenly swamped her. "For goodness' sake, leave me alone, can't you? I'm perfectly all right!"

He looked across at her mildly. "You sound it. Well, take it easy. And I'd stay away from Johnny—you aren't good for him."

It was odd, she thought, that although she knew he was right, she resented his telling her what she knew only too well herself. "I meant to go up and see him this morning."

"Go if you like. But make it a brief social call. No soul-searching, please. He does enough of that on his own. Just in and out, hello and good-bye, please!"

"That was all I was intending."

Astoundingly, Dick Clements got up and came round to her side of the big table and put his hands on her shoulders. "The day you really *mean* that, Vivien—come and tell me, will you?"

Her face was burning, and she was angry with herself for reacting to his touch. "The day I mean *what*, Dick?" She tried to move, but he held her firmly where she was and his big hands were somehow comforting.

"That your intentions are purely social, where Johnny's concerned. That you're . . ." He stopped, and took his hands away, and went back to his seat. "Oh, forget it, Viv. Sorry. I was ahead of you." He concentrated on his plate again. "Run away, there's a good girl."

She ran. She ran until she reached the wards, and went on running up the stairs instead of taking the lift. And even when she arrived outside Ward 10 she was still aware of Dick's hands, and of the fact that for the first time he had shown that he was aware of her as a person, and not only as a doctor—a subordinate at that. The small incident had shaken her more than she would have admitted to anyone. If only I could have told him about the money, she thought. He's the only person who could help, or who would really forgive me. And he's the one person I can't possibly tell.

Sister Jones was standing waiting to be noticed. "Daydreaming, Miss Bromwich? Better go in and see Mr. Dysart now, before Nurse does his dressing."

She smiled as she went to the bed, but Johnny wasn't smiling back. If anything, he looked bored. This time she didn't make the mistake of touching him. "Better, Johnny?"

He shrugged, and turned his face away. "I'm all right. There was no need for you to come."

"I *had* to. Johnny, I'm sorry if——"

"There's nothing to say, Viv. We're through. It's the end of the line. I told you."

"I know you did." She wished he would lower his voice —Sister Jones would hear every word out in the corridor. "I told myself you didn't mean it. You don't, do you?"

"For God's sake! You're behaving like a snubbed bobby-soxer! *Can't* you take 'no' for an answer? Damn it,

106

it's humiliating." He pulled the sheet up over his shoulders. "I'd have thought you'd have more pride. Most women do."

That stung. She couldn't resist a retort. "To think that Rena said you were just being noble," she burst out. "Letting me down lightly! She must be mad."

"Oh? So you've discussed it all with Rena, have you? And with half the hospital, no doubt. Even with Dick Clements." He turned his head and looked straight at her for the first time. "Yes, even with Dick. Or why are you blushing? A flush of guilt, maybe? Well, I've watched that coming for a long time. Only I never thought he was such a fool as to fall for it."

She looked back steadily into his cold eyes. "I haven't the least idea what you——"

Sister Jones's head came round the door. "Miss Bromwich! Quickly!" She beckoned and disappeared.

Vivien turned on her heel and hurried into the other side ward after the fluttering apron. But she was too late. Mr. Malcolm, his face blue-grey and his hands clawed on the sheet, was beyond any help she could give him.

She tried all the usual things while Sister Jones rang for Dick, but it wasn't any use. The hospital had lost its best consultant surgeon. That his death could complicate her own life did not occur to her, as she dismantled the useless syringe and put the coramine phial back on the tray. She was only aware of the blow the news would be to others. The full impact came when Dick Clements had come and gone in near-silence, and Sister Jones offered her a cup of tea in the linen-room.

"I was afraid of a thrombosis all night," she said. "But you know, Miss Bromwich, I never believed anything would happen. Not to *him*. He couldn't be spared so easily. It was a shock to Mr. Clements, you could see that."

"To me too, Sister."

Sister Jones leaned forward; her eyes were oddly bright above the rose-garlanded teacup. "And of course, if they find the man, it'll be murder now, think of that!"

"The man? Do they know who it was, then?"

"That I don't know. Talking, he was, to that young policeman last night. And him writing it all down in his little book. But never a word to me, Miss Bromwich. Nor to the nurses, so far as I know. Oh, it's a dreadful business!" She put down her cup. "But what about this other affair? That's what's worrying me. This money."

"It still hasn't been found?"

"Indeed, no! I had to tell Matron. And the man's the litigious kind, you see. Ready to make no end of trouble."

"Does the House Governor know?"

Sister Jones looked at her watch. "By now, likely he does. Matron was to tell him herself. Up in the theatre, that's where it went, I'll be bound. *One* of them knows something. And *not* a member of the nursing staff, if you ask me."

"Then who——?"

"I heard this morning that the porter from up there isn't on duty. Not turned up, they say. Couldn't he have taken it?"

Vivien stood up. "I don't believe anyone's taken it. I don't believe the man ever had it. He must be trying it on, Sister. Nobody here would do such a thing." And then she thought of Sister Paulson's feline eyes and hard little hands. "Or I don't *think* so."

"He had it all right. Harkness is as honest as the day. Why, he even has the numbers of the notes." She nodded. "He says he changed a lot of pound and ten shilling notes into fives at the bank just before closing time. The bank can bear it out. And it was only a few minutes later that he was knocked down, and brought straight in."

"He has the numbers? That should help. I must go, Sister. Thank you for the tea." Standing there, she suddenly heard Johnny's laugh. It seemed a long time since she had heard it. Sister Jones heard it, and looked over the side ward window.

"Very popular this morning, Mr. Dysart," she remarked. "I see he has another visitor."

Vivien looked too, curious to know whose company was so much more acceptable than her own. It couldn't have been a more unlikely person. It was the first time she had seen Nurse Haggerty smile for a long time too.

It was while she stood there that the telephone rang. The junior trotted up and looked across her at Sister

108

Jones. "It's for Miss Bromwich, Sister."

"Very well, Nurse." She looked through the window again. "Nurse, tell Staff she may as well leave Mr. Dysart's dressings till last, and do the amputation first, will you?"

Vivien picked up the dangling earpiece of the telephone. "Hello? This is Miss Bromwich."

"Vivien . . ."

He sounded so close that the effect was uncanny. He might have been standing directly behind her. "Edward!" She breathed in quickly. "Where are you?"

"Did you get the money?"

"I—— No, not yet."

"But you will?"

Although his voice was low and close to her ear, she felt that Sister Jones and the junior, and even Johnny and Staff Haggerty, must be able to hear every word. She hesitated. "Look, I can't talk here. Where *are* you?"

"Not far away, Vivien."

"But you said you were going to Manchester!"

"I know. I didn't make it."

"Then where——?"

He laughed softly. "Never mind. When you get the money, go to the telephone box at the corner of Derricourt Road—you know it?"

"Yes, I know it."

"Go there, and put the money inside the back cover of the Classified Directory—got that?—at ten o'clock, night or morning. Clear?"

"Ten o'clock," she echoed. "But how will you——?"

"I shall be watching. I shall be watching you all the time, Vivien. And by the way, if anyone wants to know where I am, what will you tell them?"

"I—I don't *know!* Nobody will want to know. Not from me."

"You'll say that I've gone to Manchester. D'you hear?"

As though it had been projected on a screen in front of her, the vision of Mr. Malcolm's bandaged head, and the sound of his voice saying, "That fellow . . ." assailed her. "Edward!" she began. "Mr. Malcolm—— Did you know that he——?" The click of the receiver at Edward's end silenced her.

She went straight to Rena after lunch, and followed her into her room. Rena's face had a queer, remote expression, and she stood at the window without turning round. "Want something, Viv?"

Vivien took a deep breath. "You said that if I were desperate—— If it was really—— That you could lend me the money."

"Did I?" Rena's voice was cool. "Rash of me! Well?"

"Well. . . . Well, *will* you?"

Rena lit a cigarette thoughtfully before she answered. Then she turned round. "Do you know, I don't think I will, after all."

"But, Rena! You *said* that——"

"Yes, I suppose we all say things we regret at times. And in the circumstances I think I'd prefer to withdraw the offer, if you don't mind!"

Vivien stared. Rena's face was as cold as Johnny's had been. She meant every word. What had happened to change her mind? "All right. I'm sorry. I wouldn't have asked you if you hadn't offered . . . and if it hadn't been really urgent. You know that. If you knew how——"

Rena blew smoke up to the ceiling. "I think you'd better go to the police, you know. Because you know where he is, I expect."

"But I don't! And why should I go to the police?"

"My good girl! You heard what we were discussing at lunch."

"I didn't hear anything. I was late coming in, and you were alone. And you scarcely spoke to me. What *were* you discussing at lunch?"

"We were discussing," Rena said very distinctly, "the fact that your little friend Featherstone—if that is his real name—is very badly wanted by the police."

"You mean—you mean they think *he* took it?"

"Took what?" Rena frowned. "I don't know what else they want him for, of course. But it was he who was trying to make off with Mr. Malcolm's car—and who managed to kill him." She swallowed. "He's wanted for murder, Vivien."

"*Murder?*" Vivien sat down suddenly on the chair behind her. "You do *mean* it? Couldn't it—couldn't it be manslaughter?"

"With malice aforethought? While committing a felony? Hardly! I would say that was murder all right. Wouldn't you?"

"But who *says* it was Featherstone?"

"Who could? Mr. Malcolm, of course. Couldn't have meant anyone else when he said, 'That fellow with yellow eyes, the new porter in the theatres', could he?"

"And that's what he said?"

"That is precisely what he said. So would you mind getting out? I never really wanted to get mixed up in this sordid little affair in the first place. Now I'm quite determined not to. What's more, if you don't take my advice and tell the police what you know, I'm quite prepared to rat on you. I have my limitations, Vivien." She stubbed out her cigarette and opened the door meaningly. "There's one little quotation you might care to think over, Vivien. 'Experience all is of use, save one, to have angered a friend.' I'm afraid I've reached the point of no return where you're concerned."

CHAPTER VIII

WALKING blindly out of Rena's room, Vivien was hardly aware of anyone going downstairs beside her until Dick Clements touched her arm. "I don't know what's biting you, Vivien—but isn't this the day you were going to work all day?"

She stopped and looked up. After her experience with Johnny Dysart and Rena, she was quite prepared to find Dick's eyes as coldly disapproving as theirs. But they were as kind as always. "Yes. Yes, that's right, Dick. Have you a job for me?"

"Not one you'll thank me for."

"I'll thank you for—for anything that will occupy my mind."

"Then I've the very thing." He hesitated, looking down at his feet. "If there's anything I can do . . . ? Well, I'm here."

She shook her head. "Thanks, Dick. There isn't. What's the job?"

"Awfully dull, but it has to be done. I want someone to go through all of the Malcolm case-papers and fish out every case of intestinal obstruction for the last four years. Can do?"

"Of course. But surely——"

He nodded. "I know. 'Any clerk could do it.' That's what you think! I want you to do it. And I want you to sort out all those that I operated on myself. Right?"

"I see!" She smiled. Obviously he was going to write a thesis. This was something personal for Dick, not just a piece of hospital statistic routine. Oddly, that made it worth while. "I get the point now. I'll do it with pleasure, if you don't need me in Cas or O.P.?"

"If I do, I'll ring." He began to go on down the stairs then, but at the bottom he stopped again, looking down at her. He looked almost nervous, she reflected. "Viv——"

"Yes, Dick?"

"You remember what I said about you and Johnny?"

"About—wanting to know when my calls were purely social?" It was new for Dick to reduce any conversation to a personal level. "Yes, I remember."

"I know now. Johnny made it very clear when I called on him. I see I was mistaken. All this time I was sure he had a—a proprietorial interest, as they call it. That you and he——"

She was astonished. "But, Dick! It couldn't have mattered less to you, one way or the other!"

"Is that the way it's looked? Then I'm more histrionically accomplished than I thought! Never mind. Forget it for now." He bent quickly to brush her forehead with his lips. "Take care of yourself, girl. And don't get cold down in the basement among the files, will you?"

She swallowed hard and stared up at him. "No, I won't."

When he had hurried away down the back path to the hospital she went on slowly to the main entrance, and collected the vault keys from the porter.

The files in the big steel cabinets went back ten years, in order of date, and there was no cross-file system to sort the cases into types, so that she had to begin on the "A" drawer and sort as she went, selecting suitable cases, and checking the notes individually, looking for: "Opn. by R.S.O." on the second page.

She stood staring at the fifth set of papers, and sat down on a packing case to think. Dick had been very clever. She read through the notes again before she put them aside and filed the other four again. With the envelope under her arm she locked the vaults, and went straight back to the Residents' House. In the common-room she sorted through the old numbers of the medical directory until she found the one she wanted. What an idiot she had been, she thought, not to have worked it out for herself.

There it was, the same name and address as that on the G.P.'s letter in the envelope she had brought back from the files. Edward Featherstone Catlow, M.D., with an address in Edgbaston. There was no mistaking the handwriting of the letter the patient had brought in. And there was no dodging the fact that three years earlier the name of Featherstone Catlow had been removed from the medical register. She checked through the lists twice to make sure. Edward was not only using a false name; he had been crossed off, three years before *crossed off the register*!

People didn't get crossed off for minor peccadilloes. It had to be something big. She thought of Edward's voice on the telephone, and shivered. She was still sitting there when Bill Stedman came over for an early cup of tea. He had never looked so dejected, but he brightened when he saw her. "Hallo, Viv. Long time since I saw you."

"Hardly, Bill. I saw you last night."

He frowned. "Oh, was that you? Sorry. I wasn't being very observant right then, I'm afraid. Didn't tread on you or anything, I hope?"

She hesitated for a moment, and then went over to face him. "Bill—could I say something awfully impertinent? Don't take it as final, that's all."

"Rena, you mean?"

113

"It's not my business, I know. Do forgive me. But I'm fond of you both, and——"

He smiled wryly. "That pretty well makes it your business, then." He began to roll up the edge of the window curtain into a tight little cylinder between his fingers. "She's said no, that's all. Finis."

"If you knew *why* she'd said no, you wouldn't take that for an answer. I just know you wouldn't. And so does she. But she's so sure it wouldn't be 'fair' to you. Bill—she said: 'He's the one.' Is that any comfort?"

Bill shot to his feet. "She *did?* Then why——?"

"You must make her tell you herself, Bill. I can't."

He beamed "Viv, I could kiss you."

"No, don't. Give me some information instead." She glanced down at the filing envelope still in her hand. "There's a G.P. I want to get hold of; he was in the directory four years ago, and now he isn't."

"Struck off, maybe?"

"Could be. How would I find out?"

"The G.M.C. would know, obviously. Or the branch of the B.M.A. he belonged to. What was his name?"

"Catlow. E. F. Catlow. He used to have an Edgbaston address. Does it ring a bell?"

Bill frowned. "D'you know—it *does*. Only I can't quite think . . . Leave it with me, Viv. It'll come to me when I'm thinking about something else. I've seen the name somewhere recently, I'm pretty sure. Can't think where, though."

With that she had to be satisfied. But she had made one mistake, as she realised when Dick rang through a few minutes later.

"Tried to run you to earth in the dungeons," he said. "Don't tell me you've knocked off already!"

"I did a few, and then——Dick, do you seriously want me to go on with it? Or was it just a gag?"

"It certainly was not! I have a paper to write on the subject by Friday, for the *Lancet,* and I must have the stuff sorted out by tomorrow at latest. Gag, indeed! Why did you think it was? Did you think I wanted you out of the way in a nice quiet sit-down job, or something?"

"Something like that, yes."

114

"Then you can think again. I want you now down in Cas. Come and help me with a couple of plaster jobs, will you?"

So Dick hadn't been so clever after all. It was quite fortuitous, finding Edward's letter. And of course, there were probably hundreds of them in the files, as there were from all the other local G.P.s, if she had cared to look. She found it strangely comforting that Dick was not, after all, aware who Edward really was.

*   *   *

He was not unaware for very long, nor was anyone else in the hospital. The evening paper carried the story on the front page. EX-DOCTOR WANTED FOR QUESTIONING, shouted the headline. And there was a picture of Mr. Malcolm, and an obituary too. But the telling paragraph was that which described the wanted man as: "Edward Catlow, *alias* Featherstone, once a practising doctor, lately a porter at the Queen's Hospital. . . ." It had not taken the police long to identify him, Vivien thought. Yet nobody at the hospital seemed to have suspected that he was not what he seemed. Except Rena. . . . Rena had known something that very first night at the dance. Rena, too, had said, "Featherstone—*if* that's his name." But whatever she had known, she had kept it to herself.

Even when the talk broke out over supper, Rena kept silent; but Dick Clements was frankly taken aback. "So *that's* who the fellow was!" he said blankly. "No wonder we thought he didn't seem quite the type. And no wonder he was so knowledgeable. Well, well. You just never know whom you're working with, do you? But how *he* could have gone for the Chief—it's a ghastly set-up. Did he have something against him?"

Roddy MacBain grunted, re-reading the paper. "Seems not. Seems the idea was to pinch the old boy's car. Anyone's would have done, presumably."

Dick shook his head. "But why did he *want* to pinch it?"

"To make a getaway, I imagine," Rena said suddenly. "There must be other charges, obviously."

115

Dick slapped his hand down, making the cups rattle. "Catlow! I remember. Some drug racket, wasn't it? Yes! Then he was up to no good here in a hospital, was he? We shall hear more about this, you mark my words. The poor old Queen's is coming in for some publicity we could well do without."

"Not necessarily." Bill flushed apologetically. "After all, he might have come here with the idea of going straight, as they say. It *was* a job he was fitted for, to be fair to him, wasn't it?"

Rena looked at him, and then dropped her eyes. "You're too nice, Bill. You don't know a scoundrel when you meet one." She stood up. "I can't stay here gossiping—I've a ward round to do yet."

So had the others, it seemed. But Dick hung back until he was alone with Vivien. "You've eaten nothing," he said. "Why not come clean? Or don't you trust me?" He took her hand and led her to the window-seat, and made her sit down beside him. For the third time his quiet strength was unbearably moving to her, the more so for its silence. He put an arm across her shoulders and waited. It was quite clear that he was prepared to wait all night, if necessary, for her to confide in him. "I'm waiting," he reminded her. "I can't see you going about looking so desperate much longer. It's getting between me and my work, that sad little face of yours, Viv. And that's something I don't allow anything to do to me."

"Then why does it?"

He smiled, and it was a smile that made hay of most of her defences. "That's a probing question, Vivien. I don't answer them. Well—going to tell me? Or shall I tell *you*?"

"Could you, Dick? I hardly think so."

He pondered up at the ceiling. "I could tell you a little, maybe. For instance, on the rebound from Johnny, you've been nursing a certain regard for this fellow Catlow. Right? And now, obviously, you feel an almighty ass. What's more——"

"What's more, I could help the police to find him— only I don't know how to bring myself to do it."

"Don't you?" Dick's face sobered, and the old harassed

116

look came back. "Then let me tell you. Can you seriously think of Mr. Malcolm—of what we've lost—in the same breath as thinking of keeping quiet if you know anything about the chap who did it? Look—I won't ask any questions, but do see that you've *got* to tell them if you know where he is."

Vivien looked at her watch. "Will you go with me? Now, I mean."

"I'll go anywhere with you, Viv. Any time you say. You may as well realise that, here and now, if it's any use to you." He stood up. "I'll get the car, and take you down to the station. Or shall I get them here?"

"No, don't get them here. Take me, will you, Dick?" Now that her mind had been made up for her she felt curiously relieved already. "Only hurry."

"You wait here." He touched her cheek gently with one finger. "Good for you, Viv." A moment later she heard him running downstairs.

When the police car stopped a hundred yards from Derricourt Road, the Inspector who sat in the back seat between her and Dick nodded at her. "Right. You take it from here. You've got three minutes before ten, so you can take your time. Got the envelope?"

She showed him the package in her hand. "Yes, it's here. I—I feel every kind of traitor."

"Then don't, miss. Feel that you're avenging that good man's death instead. That's the way to see it. Off you go."

Dick squeezed her hand as she climbed out. "We'll be with you, Viv. Don't worry."

Somehow she made herself walk steadily as far as the telephone box. The clock outside the corner stores said exactly ten o'clock as she opened the door. She slipped the envelope inside the back cover of the yellow classified directory, as Edward had told her, and closed the door again. And then she walked back towards the hospital, as the Inspector had explained that she should, without looking back.

Dick Clements caught her up before she reached the main entrance. "I didn't wait to see what happened," he told her. "Didn't want anything to happen to *you*." He fell into step with her, and then stopped. "Look, we don't

117

need to go straight back if we let them know where we are, do we? I don't need to do any rounds yet. Neither do you. Let's go somewhere different for an hour or so? Yes?"

"Somewhere else?"

"Yes. Away from it all, as it were. Do you good. You wait here, and I'll nip in and tell the switchboard where to find us if we're wanted. All right?"

"All right." She nodded. "Thank you, Dick."

She watched him race up the steps to the front hall, and waited until he clattered down again. "That's that," he said. "I've told them we'll be at the Olympia, if they want us. First, we've got to walk back for the car. It's still outside the police station. Not far."

"Ought we to go in and——"

"No," he told her firmly. "We ought not. They'll tell us, when there's anything to tell. Right now you need to think about something else. Food, for example." He tucked her arm in his. "Quick march!"

He was being very sweet, she reflected. After Edward's heady love-making, and Johnny's casual affection, he was a wonderfully safe person to be with. Safe, but exciting at the same time, and tremendously alive. Her fingers tightened involuntarily on his arm. "You're good to me, Dick. And I don't deserve it. If you knew——" She had still not explained that the money she had passed over to him for the car had come from Edward. For all that he—and the police—knew, Edward was going to the telephone box to pick up a loan. Not the repayment of one. But Dick needed the money; it would never have been fair to put him in a position where he felt obliged to return it, she told herself.

"I know all I want to know now. So suppose you calm down, and make social conversation for a change?" He smiled down at her, and hugged her arm closer. "This is a party. It's the first time we've been anywhere together, Viv. An occasion."

She fell in with his mood of determined optimism, and set out to enjoy herself.

The quiet, softly-lighted restaurant was a haven of peace, and the meal was the best she had had for weeks.

118

All through it they talked of anything and everything but the subject that was uppermost in her mind, and it was curiously exciting to be sitting there with Dick. It occurred to her for the first time that he was extremely good-looking and presentable. And she never remembered seeing him smile so often.

The blow came when the waiter brought the bill. "Lord!" Dick said. "I'm an idiot. Left my wallet in my white coat. You got any money, Viv? Lend me some, there's a dear."

"I've still got my salary packet. I haven't used any of it yet. Here." She dipped into the little envelope and fished out a five-pound note. "Change this for me."

"Thanks." He laid the note on the waiter's tray, and leaned over to help her with her coat. "Some people must be well off! Do you mean to tell me you've been carting that about for three days without spending any of it? Mine's half gone already."

"I haven't been out. They might as well pay us by cheque, the way they used to, for all the shopping sprees I have time for. I don't know why they insist on——" She looked up. The waiter was standing at Dick's elbow, and his expression was odd. "Not enough?" she asked.

"Excuse me, sir. Could you step into the manager's office for a moment?"

"What is it? Hospital want me?" Dick followed him at once, and Vivien lit a cigarette and waited. .

When he came back Dick's face was thunderous. "Come on, Viv. We'd better go."

"What is it—a flap on?" Then all the pleasant atmosphere of the past hour evaporated and she was suddenly cold with fear. "Have they—have the police found Edward?"

He shook his head as he held the swing door for her. "Nothing like that at all." When he had seen her into the car, and they had moved away into the traffic, he said jerkily, "Viv, where did you get that note? The one you lent me. In your pay, did you say?"

"Why, yes. I just took it out of the envelope." She frowned. "Why? Wasn't it genuine?"

"It was genuine all right." He fell silent until he had negotiated the roundabout and headed back towards the

119

hospital. "Yes, it was genuine. Only it happens to be one of a series of numbers the police have told these restaurant proprietors to look out for. Stolen, Viv."

"*Stolen?* You don't mean—you don't mean it's one of those Mr. Harkness had?"

"Who on earth is Mr. Harkness?"

So he still hadn't heard. "The man in Ward Ten—his wallet was taken from his clothes, he said." She told Dick the story as she knew it. "Night Sister came up and asked me about it," she went on, "since I was one of the people who'd handled his things." Then the implication hit her. "Oh, Dick! This looks as though——"

"Yes, it does, rather. You handled his clothes. You produce one of his notes from your pocket. It's awkward, isn't it?"

She was shocked by the chill in his voice. "But I swear I didn't see any money, Dick! I told you—that note came out of my pay envelope! You saw me take it out!"

"Yes. Well, we shall soon find out how it happened. The police will have heard from the Olympia by now, and they'll be coming down to the hospital, I suppose. You'd better not take any more out of your envelope until they've been, had you?"

"You're only assuming it's one of Harkness's, Dick! There must be other stolen notes listed, besides his. And some of them could easily have been amongst those the cashier's office had."

"I doubt it. The man's a car dealer, you say? Then that clinches it. The police said the notes belonged to a car dealer when they left the list at the Olympia. Besides, the bank wouldn't have *issued* notes to the cashier if the numbers were on a police list, don't you see?" He sounded tired of the whole subject.

She gripped his arm and shook it. "Dick, do you really think *I* had anything to do with it?"

"I don't know what I think." He sighed. "No, I don't. Only it's a funny affair altogether. You've had that packet on you ever since you had it, and yet—— Oh, don't let's discuss it. We're not getting anywhere."

She wanted to cry. But it wouldn't have helped. All the way back to the hospital she thought until her head ached, of Edward, and the money, and the police, and Mr. Harkness, without seeing a glimmer of sense anywhere in the whole dreadful muddle.

There was a police car outside the main entrance, and an Inspector and a constable waiting in the hall. The porter said, "I've just been ringing the Olympia for you, Mr. Clements. These—these gentlemen want to see you."

Dick nodded. "Thanks. You'd better come into the waiting-room," he told the officers. "This way."

Vivien moved forward to go with them, but Dick shook his head. "Let me see what I can do first, Vivien. You'd best wait out here while I see what the position is."

She stood there, still thinking back to Edward's voice on the telephone, until he came out of the waiting-room again and beckoned to her.

"Yes?"

He pulled a chair out for her and closed the door. "You'd better sit down, Viv. These chaps"—he looked at the two policemen—"haven't come about that note."

"They've found him?" She held on to the sides of the chair. "Is he—have they arrested him?"

The Inspector cleared his throat. "No, miss, we haven't. But when we reached the telephone box—— Tell me, miss, you didn't see anyone about, did you?"

"No, not a soul. You were there too. You must know I didn't. Why?"

"It's difficult to see the box itself, miss, round the corner under the trees. And we weren't more than fifty yards behind you; but—well, when we got there, there *was* someone inside." He looked at Dick.

"Not Edward," he amplified. "A woman. And the packet had gone."

"You mean she'd got it?"

"No, miss." The Inspector cleared his throat for the third time. He seemed to be finding it all very difficult, Vivien thought. "No, miss. It must have been taken by whoever hit her."

He was watching her face carefully, she realised. She wondered why. "How do you mean, hit her?" she asked him.

"She was unconscious, miss. Hit on the head."

"Then when she comes round she'll be able to——"

Dick bit his lip. "You don't understand, Viv. They've brought her up to Cas, and Nurse Barber identified her."

She stared up at him. "Who was she?"

"Sister Paulson."

"Sister *Paulson!* Then I was right—there *was* a tie-up between them. Inspector, I think she was married to—to Catlow."

The constable and the Inspector looked at one another. "Is that why you hit her, Miss?" the Inspector asked. "Is it?"

"Look here—you've no right to say that!" Dick told him. "You can't accuse Miss Bromwich of——"

"Miss Bromwich needn't say anything unless she wishes, sir."

"But I *do* wish!" Vivien burst out. "I went into the box and left the envelope and came straight out again! I wasn't out of your sight more than a few moment. Of course I didn't hit her. I didn't even see her. If I had I'd have told you. There's some frightful muddle, and it's closing in on me, and I don't know why. Dick, tell them about the money."

"They've already heard. They—they think it a little odd. But they're looking into it tomorrow, when the cashier's here."

"And meanwhile, what happens to me?"

"Nothing, miss." The Inspector was till looking at her. "Nothing, provided you stay here and don't leave the hospital for the time being. I'm sure you'll agree to that."

There was a tap on the door and the constable went out. He came back right away. "She didn't see anyone, sir," he said. "She conscious now, Roberts says, sir. Says she went to make a phone call, and didn't see anything or anybody."

"A phone call!" Vivien burst out. "Would she go all that way to make a phone call? When there are phones here to use, and boxes just up the road? And if she was out, and as near hospital as that, she'd have come back here and phoned in comfort."

"You think she went for some other purpose then, miss? *What other purpose?*" The Inspector's face was enigmatic

122

and hostile.

"Why, to meet Catlow. Or to get the money for him, maybe. He could have rung and told her to do that."

"Then *he* wouldn't have hit here, would he, miss?" He picked up his hat. "I shall see you in the morning, both of you. Meanwhile, please stay near the telephone in case we need you."

When they had gone Dick, without looking at her, said, "It's late. Better go to bed, Viv. I'm doing a round myself —no need for you to go up."

"I've got to go up to the theatre before I turn in. I left my notebook in the——" Then it hit her. "Dick! I know how it could have happened. The money. I never worry about leaving things in my pockets in the surgeons' room. This pay-packet has hung there at least twice. Anyone who—who wanted to, could have swopped the notes. It was open, it would have been simple!"

His eyes lost their coldness and were alert at once. "Sister Paulson, you mean?"

"It's possible, Dick. Oh, do see it—it's *possible*!" She looked up at him, willing him to believe her. "She's mixed up in this whole thing. She—she's an unscrupulous woman, Dick, I known it in my bones."

"Give me that envelope, Viv. I'll go straight down to the police with it. I can't think why they didn't ask for it anyway. And you get to bed."

He was back on her side again, she noted thankfully. She gave him the little packet, and said, "Thank you, Dick. I'm—I'm sorry to let you in for all this."

For one brief moment his arms closed about her. "If you're in it, Viv, I have to be in it too, until it works out. I'm with you." And then he had gone.

*   *   *

She looked in at the common-room before she went to her room. There was only Bill there, with his feet on the mantelpiece, deep in thought. "Ah—I wanted to see you," he said. "I've been thinking, Vivien."

"Yes?"

"Yes. Sit down a minute, if you're not in a hurry. You

123

said Rena had a reason for turning me down that *wasn't* lack of affection. Well, it wasn't that she's not free, she told me that. I knew she'd been married, but that's over. Therefore it must have been something about herself that she said 'wasn't fair' to me." He looked up. "Right?"

"I can't tell you, Bill. It's not for me to say a word. She must tell you herself."

"Quiet! There are only two possibilities, or maybe three, as I see it. One, she could have a criminal record. I dismiss that as clean daft. Two, she could have some heavy financial commitments that I know nothing of. I don't think that's true, and I wouldn't care if it were. That leaves the third. It's something to do with her health. Am I warm?"

"Go on."

"If it's her health—she's magnificently healthy, any fool can see that. So there's only one possibility left in that direction."

"Well?"

Bill swung his feet to the ground. "Tell me, Viv. Is it that we couldn't have children? It can't be anything else."

She said nothing, but she knew her face had told him. "You must ask her, Bill."

"I don't need to. I knew that before I ever proposed to her. I knew, and it made no difference. How could it?"

"She said you'd take that line."

"Then I'm right? It *was* that? Viv, you don't know what a weight that is off my mind. I'll soon talk her out of that! We'll adopt children, of course. If *she* brings them up they'll be her children. They'll be what she makes them, not little ready-made characters. Or don't you believe that environment counts for more than heredity?"

"I think it cuts two ways, Bill. Heredity provides a limited amount of raw material. Training can lick it into a limited number of shapes." She smiled. "How did you know, Bill?"

"Dick told me. He quoted it to explain away some of her frustrations one day. He was quite wrong, of course. It's not children she aches for, it's affection. And it's my job to give it to her. Wish me luck, Viv."

"I do. You know I do. Or I'd never have said a word."

"Bless you. I wish I could do something similar for *you*."

124

She sighed. "You can't. I've parted brass-rags with Johnny; I've made an utter fool of myself over someone else; and now——"

"And now, at last, you've noticed that Dick's in love with you?"

Her face burned. "Bill, you must be mad!"

"No. Just observant. A medical trait, if I may say so. He's the nicest chap I know, Viv. And you're the second nicest woman."

"Oh? What about——?" She stopped. For a second or two it had all gone out of her mind.

"What about who? Sister Paulson, I suppose? Haven't I lived that down yet?"

She got up quickly. It would be a pity to spoil Bill's new cheerfulness. "That's right," she told him lightly. "Goodnight, Bill. I'm half dead." She slipped out quickly and went to her room.

* * *

There was no sleep for her until she had heard Dick come up to his room. When he passed her door she heard him hesitate for a second, and then go on and shut his door quietly.

She switched on her bedside light and reached for her dressing-gown. Obviously he had thought she was asleep, or he would have knocked at her door to tell her what the police had said.

He opened his door at once when she knocked. "Viv! I thought you'd be asleep. It's after one o'clock. . . ."

"I was waiting for you. What did they say?"

"It wasn't what they *said*. It was what they did."

"What *did* they do?"

He put out his hand and drew her collar round her face. "You'll be cold. They went round and searched her—their —lodgings. And in the morning she'll be arrested."

"Why, Dick?"

"They found the rest of the Harkness notes, for one thing. Less those she'd obligingly planted on you. What's more, they found Catlow there."

"They've charged him?"

"He'll come up before the magistrate, to begin with, in

two days' time."

"And he had Harkness's money?"

Dick grimaced. "No. That was the point. He was there looking for it, I gathered. But the police are up to all the tricks; *they* found the stuff, and he didn't. Must have been galling for him."

"How did he know she had it?"

"Oh, it's a long story. Seems he lent two hundred that was hers, or theirs to somebody—or that's his rather thin tale. And he had to replace it when she found out, for she's quite a termagant, it seems. So he must have taken it from Harkness's clothes and given it to her. And then I suppose she heard about the numbers from Sister Jones, who can't keep her sweet mouth shut, and had to get rid of it piecemeal. That seems to be the general drift."

"Then if he took it from Harkness's clothes—Dick, he couldn't have known *known* it was there, so he must have been looking through them on spec. In other words, maybe he was in the habit of looking in pockets and so on."

"Not only pockets. They found enough drugs and instruments to stock a chemist's shop, too. Up to his old games, obviously. And she must have been in on it. Not a nice pair, Viv. I—I thought you were uncharitable when she first arrived. Evidently your feminine intuition was more reliable than we knew."

"And do they still think I hit her?"

"Not since they found his fingerprints on the door of the phone box, no. And since I told them how——"

"How what?"

"Oh, nothing," he murmured awkwardly. "I told them how vicious you really are! Go to bed, do. Goodnight, Viv."

"Goodnight, Dick. Bless you for all you've done."

"All part of the service—and that reminds me: your prospective registrarship is out."

She had forgotten all about Mr. Malcolm's promise. She jerked her mind back to the everyday routine of the hospital. "They've appointed a new consultant *already*?"

"No. But they will. So you'd better wait until we know what Johnny's doing, and then we'll see about Cas. for you."

"But Johnny's quite set on Cas. You know he is."

"Is he?" He began to close his door. Then through the crack he said: "A little bird tells me he has a very different idea. Tell you tomorrow. Now *go*, girl, before I forget myself!"

The look in his eyes sent her flying back to her room with her pulse racing.

CHAPTER IX

BREAKFAST next morning was a strange, chaotic meal. Dr. Palmer, who hardly ever had meals with the rest of them, put in his head as Vivien began to pour coffee for herself and Bill Stedman, and asked, "Clements here?"

"Still in his room, I think," Bill told him.

The R.M.O. looked at Vivien. "Maybe you can help me. I've got Glasgow on the line, wanting—— Oh, there you are, Dick." He fell back to let the R.S.O. into the room, and began again. "Look, I've got Glasgow on the line. A message from Cartwright—I can't make head or tail of it. "You'd better take it."

Dick picked up the telephone. "Put that Glasgow call through here," he told the porter. "He isn't worse, is he?"

Dr. Palmer shook his head. "No, no, I don't think so. You cope with that, then, will you? There's a good chap." He effaced himself as Rena came in.

Dick listened for a moment. "Yes, Nurse. I see." He nodded, and then frowned, and held out an arm to call Vivien over. "Description of Featherstone," he told her quietly. "How'd you put it?"

"Description of—— Why, tall, slim, dark, I suppose. Why do you ask?"

"Eye colour?"

"Golden. Amber. I don't know what you'd call it. What do they want to——"

"Shush! . . . Yes, Nurse. Golden, or amber. . . . You'll ring back? Good. How is he? Fine! Give him our good wishes." He put the telephone down on its rest slowly, and stood there with his hand still on it, thinking. Then he went over to the sideboard, with Vivien at his elbow.

"Dick!" she persisted. "What was that *about*?"

He looked up blankly. "I don't know. I just don't know. The nurse simply said that Tommy wanted a description of the chap, and that she'd ring back later." He frowned. "Fishy."

"You'll tell me what they say when they——"

"Of course." He squeezed her elbow and urged her to the table. Bill and Rena were both drinking coffee in silence, and Roddy MacBain was invisible behind the newspaper. "Let's not discuss it right now, hm?"

Vivien sat watching Rena. Her face was pale and tired, and she looked as though she had a headache. Bill was watching her too, and his kind little face was screwed up with anxiety. It was left to Dick and Vivien to make conversation, and by the time they had discussed the bacon, the marmalade and the weather the telephone rang again.

Dick shot to his feet. "I'll get it. Yes. Yes, Clements speaking." His face changed. "He *did?* It's definitely not? Good lord! Yes. . . . Yes, I will, tell him. And thank him very much. He what? . . . Oh, I see. Yes, yes. That's quite clear. Thank you, Nurse."

He turned back to the table. Rena looked up for the first time. "What's wrong Dick? Tommy not so good?"

"Tommy's fine. They're talking about letting him come back here to get fit." He sat on the edge of the table, swinging one leg, and gathered their eyes. "It's not that. Seems he knew Dr. Catlow quite well, and this fellow *isn't* Catlow!"

Vivien stared at him. "But, Dick—the handwriting was the same. This is the man who wrote in about one of your cases four years ago!"

"Could be. Could be. But still *not* Edward Featherstone Catlow. *He's* been dead for some time."

Then Rena startled them all. She stood up, trembling. "And this—this creature was his batman, and when he died he assumed his identity." Her voice crackled high. "*I* could have told you that! Do you think I wasn't horrified when I found he'd taken Dr. Catlow's two first names? And how do you think I felt when I learned he

128

had actually called himself Catlow—and even *practised* as Catlow? On the strength of two years as a medical orderly and three as a doctor's batman in the R.A.M.C. The whole thing's monstrous!" She gripped the edge of the table, and closed her eyes. Bill got his arms round her just in time before she slipped sideways into her chair.

Dick squatted at the cupboard and fished out the last of the brandy they kept there. "Here, Bill. Get this down her." He passed over the glass he had poured. "If she knew all this, why on earth didn't she tell us yesterday, when the papers——?"

"Dick, oughtn't we to tell the police?" Vivien touched his arm. "Surely they'll be glad to know?"

"I suppose so. But they've probably been told already."

Roddy MacBain had been sitting gaping at them all for a full five minutes. "You mean—the chap was only masquerading?"

"That's about it." Dick reached for the telephone again. "Get me the police, will you? Yes." He turned back to look at Vivien again. "I'm sorry about all this, Viv. It must be very painful for you."

"No. No, somehow it doesn't mean a thing. I—I don't think I've really taken it all in. I'm having to think things over again, remembering things he told me about himself. It's—it's fantastic!"

"True, though. Tommy Cartwright doesn't make mistakes. Nor Rena."

Rena was frankly sobbing in Bill's arms. Roddy, thoroughly ill at ease, made his excuses and went out of the room and Vivien went over to them. "Rena, don't, my dear. Drink some coffee, won't you?"

Rena dabbed at her eyes with Bill's big handkerchief. "I'm sorry. Not like me, is it? I'm sorry, Bill. It's all right, Viv. I've been a bit strung up lately. Can't have been easy to live with."

"We don't mind that. We just don't want *you* to be upset."

Dick clicked the telephone back on to its rest. "So that's that. I told you." He shrugged. "They knew. Ever since the name appeared in the papers they've been getting phone calls from people who say Catlow was an older man,

129

and that he's been dead some time." He sat down at the table again and held out his cup for Vivien to refill it. "Any left? My brain needs clearing."

When she brought back the cup and set it beside him, he pulled her down to the chair next his. "Viv, it must be a comfort to you in *one* way, surely? It is to me. I'd have hated to think that a member of my own profession could be such an utter bounder. Now we know that he wasn't. Don't we? At least we can be thankful about that."

"I suppose so." She nodded. "I don't know how he got away with it, though. Still, I suppose you can pick up quite a lot if you work *with* a doctor for a few years."

"Lord, yes. Enough to bamboozle the general public for a time, anyhow. So long as you didn't have to operate, it's amazing what you *could* get away with in general practice. No wonder there are so many of his cases referred here for treatment. I found no end among the files, when I sorted out the cases I wanted for my paper."

The smile in his eyes was reassuring, but Vivien was contrite at once. "Oh, Dick! I forgot to finish them. Everything seemed to happen at once, and—— Oh, I *am* so sorry!"

He smiled openly. "Think nothing of it. Actually, I was going to do them myself in any case. Only then it seemed like good occupational therapy for you. So I palmed it off your way. Not to worry." He put down his cup and looked round the table. "Well! Did *you* see Rena and Bill go out?"

"No. I was looking at you, and listening to you."

As he got to his feet he bent over her and kissed her forehead. "You go on doing just that. That suits me, Viv."

She blinked away the foolish tears that sprang to her eyes. "It suits me too, Dick. I think . . ."

"Don't think. Know. And when you do, tell me."

"I promise I will."

She watched him walk out, and listened to his footsteps going down the corridor to the front door before she moved.

* * *

130

She was down in Outpatients, with a long queue ahead of her, when she saw the newsboy bringing the evening papers, and saw the placard hanging from his bag saying: FAKE DOCTOR IN COURT. There was no question of breaking off what she was doing, and she turned back to the woman lying on the examination couch and went on with the job.

She had not reckoned with Sister Bedderidge. As she pulled up the blanket and said, "Right. That's all, Mrs. Cooney. You can get dressed again. Nurse will help you," Outpatients Sister came quietly up to the desk and bent to murmur in her ear.

"Remanded for medical enquiries," she said. She tapped her temple meaningly and nodded. "They think he's a little 'took,' as porters say."

"Bless you, Sister. I was wondering . . ."

"I guessed you would be. I saw you looking at the newspaper boy. But didn't Miss Todd say anything at lunch-time?"

"Miss Todd? She wasn't in for lunch. Why should she——?"

"She was in court, seemingly."

"She—she didn't give evidence, surely?" If Rena, who had been sent to bed for a rest by Dr. Palmer, had got up and attended the court hearing, it could only mean that she had been sent for as a witness. But as a witness to what? What did she know about—whoever he was? It was queer, Vivien thought. He hadn't a name any more. Even "Edward" wasn't his own.

"Miss Todd?" Sister Bedderidge was saying. "No, I don't think so. It doesn't say so in the paper. Just says she was there, with the House Governor. They only had him in court about five minutes before they adjourned, anyway."

"I see. Does it—does it say anything about his not being a qualified man, Sister?"

"Ah, now that was what I was going to tell you. I'd have brought the paper over, only the nurses are looking at it behind my back." Her old eyes twinkled. "I knew they were waiting to pounce on it, so I left it on my desk for them and tactfully melted away! Yes, seems that his

131

name wasn't Catlow after all. What do you think it is?"

"I can't imagine, Sister." Nervously, Vivien signalled to the next patient to go into the examination cubicle. "What is it?"

"Paulson," Sister said. "Arnold Paulson. What do you think of *that?*"

Vivien stared. "So they *are* married?" She tried to focus on the case-papers in front of her. "I knew it."

"*Married?* Him and Theatre Sister? Oh dear, no! Brother and sister, that's what they are, Miss Bromwich. Fancy, none of us could have guessed that, could we? I must go, and let you get on." She bustled over to the door. "*She* was bailed out," she added, and then smiled officially and said, "Thank you, Doctor!" as she went out into the waiting hall.

Nurse Dawkins was waiting impatiently beside the couch. "Mrs. Woolley is in a hurry, Doctor," she reproved Vivien, as she jerked back the cubicle curtain. "She has to go home and meet the children from school."

"I'm sorry. Let's see—you had your operation when?"

The thin girl on the couch calculated. "Seven weeks ago, Doctor. But I don't feel right a bit. Ever so painful sometimes."

While Vivien's fingertips were at work, palpating the tense abdominal muscles, she talked, to get Mrs. Woolley to relax. "Yes, I expect it's a bit dangerous, letting the little ones cross roads alone. I'll be as quick as I can."

"Oh, it's not the roads, Doctor. They're old enough to know their kerb drill and all that. Only I worry about them being attacked, or something. Especially after that case this week—that Mr. Malcolm. Here! Isn't he the one that did my operation? Isn't it *him?*"

"I'm afraid so, Mrs. Woolley. . . . Let your muscles go loose now, or I can't find what I'm looking for. That's better. Yes, he will be a terrible loss to us."

"Oh, *dear!* And him such a nice kind chap too, Doctor. Ever so kind to me, he was. What a terrible thing! And one of the fellows from here too!" Her pale eyelashes fluttered. Just like Nurse Haggerty's, Vivien reflected. And then she sheered away from that line of thought, remembering Johnny's sudden laughter, and Staff Haggerty sitting at his bedside. "Dr. Catlow, that used to be down this way a year or two back."

"Does that hurt?" Vivien interrupted sharply.

"Yes. Yes, that's ever so tender, Doctor. What is it?"

"It's what we call adhesions, after your operation. It happens sometimes; part of the healing process that goes a bit too far. Now look, Mrs. Woolley, I want you to come up again in a week's time if the pain doesn't improve. And we *may* have to order you some special treatment from the physiotherapy department. Or we may even have to take another look inside, though I hope not." While the woman still stared up at her she added, "And no, it isn't Dr. Catlow. He never *was* Dr. Catlow. You weren't a patient of his, were you?" She bent over the case-paper and wrote a brief note.

"No, I wasn't." Mrs. Woolley sat up, and began to climb from the couch. "But my sister's husband used to go to him. Swore by him, he did. . . . Doctor, you don't really think I'll have to have another op, do you? Honestly?"

Vivien managed a smile. I hope not. But it depends how you go on."

So Mrs. Woolley's brother-in-law "swore by" Edward, did he? It was just as Dick had said: you *could* bamboozle people for a time, given enough superficial knowledge. And of course he would have had a wonderful bedside manner, that was obvious. Edward, she thought. Even that wasn't true.

While she saw the rest of the patients, and listened to those who commiserated about "poor Mr. Malcolm", she wondered again why Rena had gone to the hearing, and just how much she had known about—Arnold Paulson.

When she went over, late, for her tea, Bill was alone in the common-room at the Residents' House. He looked happier than he had done for weeks, and jumped up to pour tea for her.

"It's an ill wind . . ." he said, beaming.

Vivien looked up, puzzled. "You mean—you mean you and Rena have got together again?"

"I think so." He nodded, and brought her cup to her, and sat down opposite her at the long table. "I think so,

133

Viv. You see, she'd never really *needed* me before. Not till she cracked about this chap Catlow or whoever he is."

"Not Catlow, Bill. Arnold Paulson." Even now the name came awkwardly.

"Yes, well. She's always been so damned self-sufficient, has Rena. So tough. She never needed me—or anyone else. Did she? I was afraid she never would. I mean, I'm not much of a ladies' man; I'm no caveman type."

"She's always needed someone, Bill. Only she wouldn't admit it, even to herself. And I'm glad it's you. All fixed up now, are you?" She drank some of her tea, and was surprised to find how badly she had wanted it.

"Well, not in so many words. But I did get at her over the question of—of children."

"I'm glad." Everything was going well for everyone else, she thought. "I hope you've convinced her."

He hesitated. "I *think* so. Only I'm not yet really sure. She said that she had an awful lot of back history to explain to me before she let me 'involve myself with her life', as she calls it. I'm—I'm taking her out to dinner tonight, to try to get it settled once and for all." He smiled gently. "Not that any amount of 'back history' will make any difference to *me*. But she seems to want to come clean."

"Then let her. Maybe it's what she's needed to do for a long time. Rena is—well, not secretive, perhaps, but too bottled up. And there's an awful lot of femininity squashed into the background through putting her work first for the last ten years. She's tremendously attractive, Bill. And all that, it needs outlet. So don't shut her up if she wants to talk about herself. It's time she *did*."

"I know. I shall listen. Only all I'm saying is, that it won't make any difference. If she was a mass-murderess it wouldn't make any odds, so how can anything else?"

Then Vivien thought of something. "Haven't you forgotten one small thing, Bill?"

"Have I? Oh, you mean the ring?"

"It never even entered my head! No, not that, Bill. You say you're going out to dinner tonight? I thought it was your night for Cas?"

"It is. But I've got round MacBain."

Vivien didn't attempt to hide her surprise. "That's a

change. He doesn't take a very good view of standing in for people, as a rule. In fact, I wouldn't hesitate to say he likes a quiet life!"

"Ah, but that was before the softening-up process began."

"*What* softening-up process? Has Dick been lecturing him?"

Bill grinned. "Evidently you're behind the times with the latest night-duty rumours, Viv! They've been obscured by all this other business, I suppose. Seems Mac has entered a new phase—Operation Grover, I fancy."

"Nurse *Grover?* In the theatre, you mean?"

"So I gather. She's a nice child. May do him good."

Vivien thought of Nurse Grover's kind, round face and curly brown hair, and agreed. "She is. Very sensible, too. Well! You've surprised me, Bill! It's really a thing, is it?"

"Oh, yes. That's to say, they've been out together about three times, which is said to be something new for both of them. Anyhow, it's working miracles with Mac, so may it continue." Bill got up to go. "He *offered* to stand in. I was going to ask *you*, as a matter of fact."

"I'd have done it with pleasure."

"Well, nice of you. But now you can have a free evening instead."

Dick was in time to hear that, as he passed Bill in the doorway.

"And what will you do with your free evening, Vivien?"

She flushed uncomfortably. "Oh—potter, I suppose. Wash my hair, or something."

"Rubbish! Your hair's very nice as it is. Nice and sleek. It'll go all wild if you wash it. Besides . . ." He reached for a sandwich and went over to the window, and looked out as he munched.

"Besides—what, Dick?"

He swallowed. "Besides, I had a better idea."

"You want me to stay on duty? All right, Dick, I don't——"

"Dear idiot!" His smile broadened. "No, I want you to come out with me. No?" He swung round to face her. "No?"

She was startled. "Go out with you? But——"

135

"But nothing. I'd have asked you to long ago, only I was busy making sure about Johnny. And now I have. Lord. I tried everything. Offered you a job with him in Cas; dragged you up to the theatre when he had his op; and pumped him too."

"Oh, Dick, I *told* you it wasn't going to work, Johnny and me."

"Ah, but you weren't in your right mind just then. Now may be you are. Anyhow, will you come, that's the point?"

There was only one answer. "Yes, I'll come. Thank you."

"Any more rounds to do?"

"No, I don't think so. I'll ring through to the wards and check, though."

"Then you do that, and then wash your face and powder your nose, and I'll be ready."

"Where are we going? I mean—what do I wear?"

"Whatever you happen to dress for, that's where we'll go." He came across to her at last, and took her by the shoulders, and his face sobered. "We've a deal of talking to do, you and I, Viv," he said gently. "Just dress for that. You always look good to me, whatever you wear. Even," he smiled, "in size eight theatre boots!"

"That's one nice thought," she said, a little bitterly. "At least Sister Paulson won't be able to do me out of my 'little boots,' as she calls them, any more!"

* * *

They cruised the city centre, looking for a parking place. "Just remembered," Dick said. "Patient of mine promised me a free dinner when I could find a moment to have it." He swung into Barwick Street, and eased the car into a gap in the row along the pavement. "This is as good a time as any to call his bluff."

"Oh? Who? And won't he mind my——?"

"He won't. You'll be included, I imagine. He's the manager of the Splendide. They've just opened a new dining-room or grill-room or something. Yes?"

"Will I do in this suit?"

He looked down at her thin green tweeds and the yellow shirt blouse. "If you won't, they can keep their dinner! Of course you will. This grill-room affair is the kind of place lots of people go after a day in town. They don't dress. You look—you look wonderful, Viv."

"Thank you. I—I rather thought we might be going out into the country for a drive. That's why I—"

His face was all concern at once. "Dearest, would you rather have——" And then he flushed brilliantly under the street-lamp. "I mean——"

"You——" Vivien was speechless. He had called her "dearest". Dick! Dick Clements, of all people! Dick, who never said anything he didn't mean.

He took her arm firmly. "Let's go and eat," he said hurriedly.

*   *   *

They had no more talk until Julian Howes, the manager of the Splendide, was quite sure they had eaten to capacity. He scarcely left their table until Dick ordered coffee, and even then he lingered to reassure himself. "You really have had a good dinner, sir? And you, madam?"

Dick grinned up at him. "Wonderful, Julian. Especially the steaks. They were superb. Weren't they, Viv?"

"Heavenly. I wish we had your chef at the Queen's!"

"I'll make you a promise, madam. When you and Mr. Clements here have an occasion for celebration, when you give a big party there, then I will lend him to you!"

"I may take you up on that one day, Julian," Dick told him easily. But his cheekbones were pink with embarrassment. "Very generous of you!"

Julian nodded amiably. "Then you will let me know, madam?" He scanned their table for the last time, and bowed his way from the alcove.

"Celebration, indeed!" Vivien expostulated. "What does he think——?"

Dick reached across the table for her hand. "I don't care what he thinks? Vivien, there something I want to say to you."

She trembled at the touch of his firm warm fingers.

137

"Yes, Dick?"

"I've waited an awfully long time to say it, because I had to be sure. And now that I am, I don't know how to begin."

"Don't, Dick!" She pulled her hand away, suddenly afraid. "Don't say anything you may regret."

"Regret? Never. I know you now. I know everything I want to know about you. What I don't know isn't important. And——"

"But it is!" She clasped her hands in her lap, and struggled for the courage to tell him. "Dick, the money I paid you for the car——"

He was staring at her. "Yes?"

"I—I borrowed it from Edward . . . from Paulson."

"You—?" He looked down at his coffee and stirred it violently. "So that's it." His voice was bleak. "So *that* was why he had to steal from Harkness? Oh, *Vivien!* Then what they said was true all the time?" He looked up again, and his eyes were full of misery. "It was true—is that what you want to tell me?—that you were—that you were having an affair with him?" His hand stopped moving, as he waited.

"Dick, I've got to be honest with you. I've *got* to be. Don't you see?"

"Because——"

"Yes?"

"Oh, because I can't *not* be, Dick. Not now!"

He put the spoon down carefully in his saucer and considered the vase of carnations between them for a long time. Then he took a deep breath. "Look, Viv," he said very quietly. "I have to say this, no matter how it works out now. I brought you here tonight to tell you that I love you. I think maybe I always have, only other things got in the way. And I want you to marry me. If that isn't what you want too, say so *now*."

"I don't know, Dick. I don't know. It's too soon. And I want you to understand about—about Paulson, and everything."

"Can't you see I don't want to hear it, Viv? I don't want you to tell me. It's the last thing I want to hear. I only want to know that—whatever it was—is *over*. Viv! Please!"

"Yes, it's over," she told him dully. "It never was anything but—some madness that got into me. And you *did* know, Dick, because you told me you knew I had made an ass of myself, and——"

"I never knew you'd taken money from him!"

"What difference does that make? Oh, you men! Money is so important to you! It's more real to you than people! You know why I took it? To make it right with you over the car. So as not to worry Johnny. Not for *myself*."

Dick hid his face in his hands for a long moment. When he sat upright again he had obviously won some battle with himself. "All right, Viv. Let's forget it. I can't pretend I don't mind, because I mind like hell. But let's forget it. Maybe I'm being abominably masculine and small-minded. I don't know. What I *do* know is that— well, that for me it's you, and nobody else will do. What about you? Am I just—just another chap? Or what?"

"No, you're not. I swear. Only I'm not ready to talk about it, Dick."

"I see. Do you think you ever will be?"

She nodded. "Yes. But—— Oh, Dick, I do love you. At least I think I do. But while this trial is hanging over all of us, I *can't*——"

At once his face was alight and alive. "Viv—you know what you just said? You meant it?"

"Of course I meant it!"

"Then nothing else matters. Does it?" He stood up and came round the table to help her with her jacket. "Let's get out of here, Viv. Let's go somewhere where I can convince you."

But they got no further than the lounge. There they were waylaid by Bill Stedman, anxious-faced. "Have either of you seen Rena?"

Vivien shook her head. "You said you were having dinner with her."

"She hasn't turned up yet. She's nearly an hour late."

Dick frowned. "*I* told her to stay in bed for a couple of days. But I hear she went to that damned hearing at the court today. How come?"

Bill shrugged. "I don't know. She didn't say she intended to. And she—she doesn't seem to have been seen since. I just took it she'd turn up here, as she'd promised. She doesn't break promises. Not Rena. Do you think—?"

"I don't think anything. We'd better get back and see whether she's landed back at the House. Hadn't we?"

"I've just 'phoned. And she hasn't."

"Then we go to the last place she was seen, and begin from there. The police court. Right?" Dick looked at Vivien. "You think so?"

"I—I suppose so. But I think I know where she may have gone."

"Where?"

"She could have gone to Mr. Malcolm's house. To collect her case-notes and things, and take back those of his that she'd borrowed. They were pretty friendly."

"That's right," Bill nodded. "She could have done that. Why didn't I think of it? Only last night she was saying that she had some things to collect before the executors got cracking. And it's the funeral tomorrow, remember."

"Then telephone there," Dick said. "I suppose he'd a housekeeper or something in charge who'll know whether Rena's been there or not?"

They waited outside the telephone kiosk in the hall until Bill came out again. "No reply," he said. "So that's that."

Suddenly one of Vivien's rare hunches came to her. She had learned to follow them up. "Bill," she suggested. "You stay here, and Dick and I will cast about for an hour on our own. Will you?"

"Sure. But you'll come back, will you? Or telephone?"

"One or the other," she promised. "Is that all right with you, Dick?"

"Of course. Let's go, then." Outside in the street he stood still and looked down at her. "You've had an idea, that's plain. What is it?"

"I think she *is* at Mr. Malcolm's. She's always said how lovely and peaceful it is out there. And if she was all to pieces she'd——"

"Then why didn't she answer the phone?"

"That's what I want to find out, Dick. That's what's worrying me!"

She didn't know what she had expected, but she had certainly not imagined that they would find Rena sitting in the middle of Mr. Malcolm's drive, shivering and white-faced. Dick slammed on the brakes as the headlights picked up the flash of Rena's light scarf, and said, "What the hell——?"

Vivien got to her first. "Rena! What happened?"

"Thank God you've come. I thought nobody ever would, and that I'd still be here in the morning! Lord, I feel so ghastly." She leaned heavily on Vivien's shoulder. "I don't know how I did it, or how long ago. It seems like a year. But I fell over some piece of rockery or something. I'm afraid I've fractured a tib. and fib. Idiotic thing to do."

Then she fainted and Dick lifted her in his arms. "Let's get her into the car while she's out," he suggested. "Open the back door, Viv."

They made her comfortable on the big back seat, and covered her with rugs, before she opened her eyes again. "Taking you straight back to Queen's", Vivien told her. "Don't talk now, Rena. Dick, stop at the first telephone you see. We must ring Bill."

"Is he still waiting?" Rena asked. "Poor Bill, I thought by now he'd have given me up. What brought *you* here?" She winced with pain as the car began to move. "Nobody knew I was——"

"I guessed," Vivien told her. "Now be quiet."

"Wanted to look at the place again . . . must tell Bill. . . ." Rena's voice faded out again.

There was a telephone box, an A.A. one, at the first crossroads, and Vivien rang Bill at the Splendide straight away. "And ring Cas and tell them," she suggested. "We'll be there in half an hour. We're going slowly, so as not to jolt her."

"Good enough," Bill agreed. "You're sure she's all right?"

"Sure, Bill. Don't worry."

"Take care of her, Viv."

"Of course, Bill." His anxiety was obvious. "You can trust us, you know! We shan't neglect her!"

But he had already rung off.

141

Rena was very quiet on the way back to the Queen's. Once she said, "It's a heavenly place, Viv." That was all.

It was not until after eleven o'clock, when she was safely warded, with her leg temporarily splinted pending a morning X-ray, that they put Rena out of their minds for a moment and realised that Bill had not eaten since tea-time. Dick said: "Leave it to me, old man. I'll go and brave the kitchen for you."

"You haven't a hope, if Winnie's gone to bed," Vivien told him. "Tell you what—why not beg from the night nurses? They always have a few spares left out."

"That's a thought. One way of getting something hot," Bill agreed. "Don't you people bother. I'll go and see my favourite night nurse."

Vivien smiled. "And who might *that* be?"

"Don't tell a soul!" Bill held up a finger to his lips. "It's little Nurse Gourlay, on women's medical."

They all laughed, and it eased the tension of the last few hours. "Indeed?" Dick said. "Baby-snatching, is it? She can't be a day over twelve, by the look of her."

"It's a base lie," Bill told him. "I know for a fact that it was her nineteenth birthday last Friday. She asked me to her party!"

"Why didn't you go?"

"Frankly, because I'd be terrified of all those girls *en masse*. One at a time is all I can cope with. Anyhow, I'm sure she'll find me something to eat."

He wandered off, and Dick took Vivien's hands in his.

"Viv, our evening went off the rails a bit, didn't it? I was just going to take you——"

"Somewhere where you could convince me?" she asked. "I know. But I have to convince myself. And I have to see Johnny just once more too. Let me do this my own way, Dick. Please."

"Why Johnny? Now? At this stage? Viv, are you still hankering after him? Aren't you sure of yourself even now?"

She took her hands away from him. "Don't let's say any more just now, Dick. Don't let's spoil it all."

"Then let me say just one thing. And I mean it, Viv. By tomorrow you've got to make up your mind. This has

142

been getting in the way of my work too long. I can't do my job properly until I know where I stand. Do *see* that. My work matters more to me than anything——"

"More than I do?"

He thought about it carefully, frowning. "As much, I think. Yes, Viv. It matters as much as you do."

"And if you had to choose?"

"I don't know. That's the kind of choice a man hopes he'll never have to make, Viv. You must know that. Look, I'm trying to be honest. I can't give you flowery talk, I'm not that kind. I can only be truthful. Now, good night." He leaned forward and kissed her lightly on the cheek. "Make up your mind by tomorrow, Viv. Be fair to me. And remember that I love you."

When he had gone out of the room she burst into tears. It was Roddy MacBain who pushed a clean handkerchief into her hand ten minutes later.

"Anything I can do?" he wanted to know.

She shook her head and mopped her eyes. "Not a thing, thanks. I'm tired, I suppose. You heard about Rena, of course?"

"Didn't I see her in Cas?"

"Of course. I must be wandering. I just wondered what she was doing out there. Whether she'd said anything."

"Out at The Hill? Looking around, she says. Only the housekeeper wasn't in, and——"

"And what?"

"And it's time you went to bed, Vivien. Go on, clear off. You look all in. I've got rounds to do yet, and I'm not going until you go upstairs. So——"

She smiled waterily. "All right, Roddy. Thanks. Theatre working?"

"No." He flushed. "Why?"

"I wondered whether Nurse Grover was on duty. Because an hour ago you said you'd finished your rounds!"

"Oh, so you've heard about that, have you?" He grinned. "I must say news travels fast in this place. No, she isn't on. But I do tend to prowl about hoping for a case to materialise. Daft, isn't it?"

"No, not if it makes you happy. Does it?"

It was the first time he had looked thoroughly alive, she

143

thought. His eyes had a new alertness and his mouth had lost its droop. "Yes," he nodded. "Yes, I think it does. We shall see. She's—very sweet."

"I know. Now go to bed."

Vivien nodded. "She's one of the nicest girls on the staff as a matter of fact. You're very lucky."

She went up, but it was a long time before she slept. She lay watching the headlights of the passing traffic making patterns on her ceiling, and thinking round in the same circles over and over again. But when she had heard Dick's door close, and the click of his light switch, she closed her eyes. Tomorrow she would make up her mind. Not tonight.

CHAPTER X

VIVIEN woke with a throbbing headache on the morning of Mr. Malcolm's funeral. By the time she opened her eyes she knew exactly why. "Tomorrow," Dick Clements had said. "Make up your mind tomorrow." Yet only a week ago he had said, "When you know, tell me." Already he was finding that his feelings for her distracted him from his work. Johnny had never told her that she spoiled his work. Nor had Edward. But there wasn't any Edward, she remembered. There was only a perfect stranger named Arnold Paulson.

She got out of bed, her head thudding, and washed her face in cold water in an effort to clear her muddled thoughts, but she was clear about only one thing: she had no intention of going in to breakfast. Not only was the thought of food nauseating, but also breakfast meant meeting the others, Dick among them. She had to have time. Time to think.

Then she remembered Rena, lying in Ward 9 with her fractured leg under a big cradle. Instead of going into breakfast she would go up and see Rena before the day nurses came on duty.

Nurse Wentworth was hurriedly finishing her report, half sitting, half standing, at the ward table, with her cap askew from the rush of the morning routine.

Vivien put her head round the door. "May I see Miss Todd, Nurse? Or isn't she ready?"

"Yes, of course, Miss Bromwich. Do her good to see you, I expect. She's had quite a decent night, but she's getting a bit restless now." She hesitated. "Do you mind if I——"

"No, you carry on, Nurse. It's purely a social call. I'm not doing a round at this hour!"

In the side ward Rena was moodily brushing her hair, but she lit up at once when she saw Vivien. "Oh, Viv! How nice of you to come so early. The nurses are dear, sweet girl, but I do find their conversation the littlest bit monotonous!"

Vivien smiled. "I expect the poor dears are scared stiff of you. A senior houseman in the side ward must be a bit of a bind. They expect you to be critical, even if you're not." She sat down beside the bed. "How do you feel?"

"Stiff. And I've a ghastly cold too. But bless you for coming and finding me. I'd have been there until morning if you hadn't. The housekeeper was a daily, you know. He didn't like people living in." She sighed. "It's the funeral today. And I can't go."

"No, nor can I. Dick's the only one going from the House, apart from the R.M.O. and the House Governor and Matron. No time. Do you mind not going?"

"I mind terribly. I'm the one person who should be there. Viv . . ."

"Yes?"

"Viv, I'm not supposed to know. At least, it isn't considered the thing. Only he told me, you see. . . . Do you *know* what he's done?"

"What?"

"I never thought a thing about it, because it seemed so awfully remote at the time. He—he's left everything he has to me!"

"Rena! Everything? Hadn't he any family?"

Rena shook her head. "Nobody very close. He said I was as close to him as anyone, even when I——"

"Turned him down?"

"Something like that. I can't take it in, you know."

Vivien leaned across and kissed her cheek. "I'm so glad for you. As they say in the Westerns, it couldn't have happened to a nicer guy. I only hope it brings you some of the things you want."

That made Rena laugh. "Oh, Viv! You know darned well money *never* gets you what you really want. Or hardly ever. And that lovely house too, and all the animals. Peace. He's left me *peace*, Viv. That's the thing. Rest and peace and all those things that I've never somehow had."

Vivien said carefully, "What about Bill, Rena?"

"I'm afraid—I'm afraid this may make a difference." Rena looked up, and her eyes were bright with tears. "You know Bill, Viv. When he finds out about all this— how will he feel? He'll want to back out, in case someone thinks he's after my money. He's as—as sweet and daft as that."

"Oh, Rena! Everyone knows Bill's adored you for long enough. Before ever this happened. And he's not likely to back out if *you* love *him*. And you do, don't you?"

"Yes," Rena admitted simply. "I do. So much that I've had to give way on every point—even over what I told you."

"Then give way on this by letting him see how you feel. He doesn't know yet, then?"

"Not yet. I was waiting for him to come up this morning. He's bound to say, 'Why were you looking around at The Hill?', isn't he? And that's my cue." She smiled. "Poor Bill—I know he'll be stunned."

"He'll be glad for you, Rena. You deserve so many things you haven't had."

"Do I? I doubt it. Listen, Viv. There's something else I want you to know too. I want to tell you about Paulson. I feel horribly guilty, because I ought to have told you before you got involved. Only how was I to know how deeply you *would* be involved? I blame myself, be-cause——"

Sister White's head came round the door. "Good morn-ing, ladies. You're early, Miss Bromwich! Not a round yet, I hope?" She came in with her temperature book,

146

and unhooked Rena's chart. "Yes, I see. I think you've chattered long enough, don't you?" She looked sharply at Vivien. "You all right, Miss Bromwich?"

Vivien pulled herself together enough to say, "I'm all right, Sister," and then the throb in her head mounted unbearably, and as her face burned she felt herself begining to shiver. "At least . . ."

"At least you are running a temperature?" Sister White's voice sounded a long way off, but her dry, warm hand was very near and solid as she pushed Vivien down into a chair. "Nurse! Nurse, come here, will you?"

Two minutes later Nurse Wentworth was wheeling Vivien to the lift in a wheel-chair, swaddled in red blankets.

*   *   *

It was late afternoon when she opened her eyes dizzily and found herself in her own bedroom. There was a post-card on her bedside table that said: *Ring Home Sister when you wake, please.* But it was a long time before she was orientated enough to lift the receiver, and the very touch of the cold plastic set her shivering again.

It's 'flu, she thought, and somehow that was amusing. She was still giggling feebly when Home Sister came in. "Such a stupid thing to have," she said. "Why *now*?"

Home Sister pushed a thermometer into her mouth and smiled grimly. "I saw it coming, Miss Bromwich. You never gave yourself a chance to get over the shock of that accident. Running about too soon, and see where it's got you! And no doubt you got cold yesterday, bringing Miss Todd back from Mr. Malcolm's."

"How did you know?"

Sister laughed shortly. "There's not much goes on in this place that *I* don't hear, my dear. No, not much, I can tell you. I've been here a long time. I know all the signs. Whether it's housemen flirting with night nurses, or house-women catching cold, or——" She looked critically at the thermometer. "Hm! Or porters who are nothing of the sort," she finished. "I hear it all, one way and another."

Vivien wondered whether she knew about Rena's legacy.

147

"Could I have a drink, Sister? Tea, or something like that?"

"You can have hot lemon, Miss Bromwich. I'll bring it myself. I don't want Winnie down with 'flu, thank you. We're short enough of labour as it is." She nodded. "You've seen your flowers?"

"No." Vivien twisted her head, heavily, to look across the room. There were great golden chrysanthemums in a tall vase, glowing in the sunset light. "Oh, lovely." She remembered the red roses Edward—no, Arnold—had sent her. These were so much more wholesome-looking. "Who from, Sister?"

"I don't know. Staff Nurse Haggerty brought them over. There's a card, I think." Sister went over to look. "From Mr. Dysart." She flipped Vivien a strange little look. "I thought so. He's out of the ward, you know. Going on sick leave until they can finish his hand. Maybe he'll be in to see you later on."

"Already?"

"You can't keep an active young man in bed every long, Miss Bromwich. Particularly when he's a doctor who thinks he has a charmed life. It's easier to let him get up and find out how he feels, than to try to control him in bed. I'll get your drink."

Flowers from Johnny. What did that mean? she wondered. Not every much, if Staff Haggerty had brought them over. On the other hand, what was it he had said about her? "Those rabbit's eyes," he had remarked. But then he had said, "The best theatre staff nurse we've ever had."

She drank the lemon drink Sister brought her, and settled into an uneasy doze again. And then the door opened softly, and Dr. Palmer said, "Are you awake, my dear?"

When she moved he snapped on the bedside light and stood smiling down at her. "Feeling a little better?"

She nodded. "Stupid of me. I'll be all right tomorrow."

"*This* time you'll oblige me by having a proper rest, young woman!" He took her wrist lightly, feeling her pulse. "Yes, a proper rest. I'm not so short of staff that I want them on duty in this state."

In the moment of clarity that his cool fingers seemed to

bring she asked, "Did you go to the funeral?"

He nodded. "Yes. It was curiously quiet and simple for such a celebrity. It didn't seem to me that his passing had been marked at all. It was all rather like an informal little visit to an old friend, you know."

"That's how it should be," Vivien said hazily. "I hate ostentation, don't you?"

"Exactly," said the R.M.O. "Exactly. Well, rest now. I shall see you tomorrow. Anything you need?"

"I don't think so. Unless——"

"Yes?"

"Could you pass me the card from the flowers?"

"Of course. What magnificent chrysanthemums! I used to grow them before I came here. Great fun to potter with. Wonderful excuse to go out and waste time in the garden shed! There you are. Anything else?"

She took the card and lay flat again. "No, thank you. I expect Night Sister will come over later." She frowned. "How is it I wasn't warded?"

"No beds! And it seemed a good idea to keep your nasty little virus out of the wards. Seven nurses went down today too." He opened the door, and sketched a wave. "Good night, then."

"Good night. And thank you." She managed a thin smile.

Johnny didn't come, and didn't come. And when Night Sister came over at half-past nine she found Vivien tossing feverishly. "I'll sponge your hands and face," she promised. "You *have* got yourself into a stew!" She went over to the basin and ran warm water.

"Lovely to lie back and *be* washed," Vivien said gratefully. "I can't think why the patients grumble."

Sister smiled, and began to dry her face gently. "Maybe some of the nurses are not very handy! I've been at it a long time, remember."

"You're very gentle. Nice to be a baby, now and again."

"Oh?" One of the perfect eyebrows went up a quarter of an inch. "And just what are you running away from, Miss Bromwich?"

Vivien was startled. "I? Running away?"

149

"Aren't you?" Sister folded the towel and hung it neatly on its rail. "Sounded like it to me!"

"Oh, Sister! You're as bad as Home Sister. *She* says she doesn't miss anything."

"Well, it's what we're trained to do, after all. Observe. Know how people tick. Help when we can. No?"

"Yes. But you *can't* help half the things you observe."

"No. Life's like that. Well now, a drink and some codeine. Feel like anything solid? No. Like a visitor?"

"Is—is the R.S.O. in?"

"In the theatre, right now. A job after his own heart too. A nice little strangulated hernia. He won't be over just yet. Anyone else?"

"No. But give my love to Miss Todd, won't you, Sister? If she's awake."

"She'd better not be awake! She's had so many visitors that she had to have a dose of seconal tonight to sleep on." Sister shook her head. "She had Mr. Dysart, Mr. Clements, Mr. Stedman, Mr. MacBain *and* the R.M.O. Holding a regular court. I hope you don't expect to do the same?"

"No, I don't feel up to that." So Johnny and Dick had both been to see Rena, and not been in to see her. It was all very fine to talk about carrying virus; they could at least have put their heads in for a moment, she told herself. For the second itme she looked at the card Johnny had sent with the flowers. *Get well soon, J.D.*: that was all it said. Dick hadn't sent any message at all.

Sister came and went, brought a drink and tablets, and arranged a green scarf over the bedside lamp. And then Dorothy, the housemaid, tapped and opened the door. "Miss Bromwich," she hissed. "Can I come in?"

"Yes, Dorothy. Don't come close to me, though. You mustn't catch my 'flu, must you?"

"Oh, I'm not afraid of those things, miss. Look, I got a little parcel for you. Couldn't bring it before." She dumped the queer-shaped package on the bed and bolted.

There was a mass of tissue paper, and then a plant-pot emerged, with nothing in it but a very ugly little cactus plant. But there was a note with it. A note from Dick. It said, *I told you I wasn't a flowery person, Viv. Like this cactus in a way. I'm told the bloom is imminent—hope*

150

that's an omen. Don't forget me. Dick.

The funny, ugly little plant certainly had a sturdy bud at its tip. She smiled at it, and set it carefully on the table, before she put out the light. Evidently Night Sister's codeine was taking effect. It was the first time her head had stopped aching since early morning.

* * *

Two days later she woke, clear-headed at last, in the middle of the afternoon. Staff Nurse Haggerty stood unblinking at the foot of the bed.

"You're better, Miss Bromwich?"

"Yes, I'm better, thank you. But——" She struggled to sit up.

"Oh, I know I shouldn't be here in the House, but I promised Mr. Dysart I'd come and see you."

Vivien was stung. "Why doesn't he come himself, Staff?"

"He's gone away, Miss Bromwich. On sick leave." She walked calmly round the bed and took the chair at the far side. "I always think it's best not to beat about the bush," she remarked. "You'll be wanting to know his plans, I dare say."

"He—he *sent* you to see me?"

Haggerty shrugged. "I said I'd come. You were sleeping when he left. I told him I'd explain to you."

"Explain what? What is there to explain?"

The colourless, efficient eyelashes fluttered once, and were still. "Mr. Dysart has decided to take a radiology course when he's well enough. That seems to offer a worth-while future. Meanwhile . . ."

She was pausing for effect, Vivien told herself. She closed her eyes and lay back. "Well?"

"Meanwhile I shall go on working. I've been promoted Theatre Sister, and the pay will be much better. We plan to marry when it's possible, you see. When he has a radiology post."

Vivien's eyes flew open. "You—you and Mr. Dysart plan to marry? Just like that? Rather a sudden decision, isn't it?"

"Not as far as I'm concerned. And surgeons learn to

take quick decisions, don't they?" Haggerty stood up again and replaced the chair neatly under the edge of the bed. "You were entitled to know."

"Yes, Staff, I think I was." Suddenly laughter overcame her, a gale of laughter, and then she thought, I'm hysterical, it isn't funny at all, and struggled to control her breath. "I hope you'll be very happy," she said politely. "You seem to have it all worked out."

Haggerty, at the door, nodded soberly. "Oh, yes. It doesn't do to plunge into things haphazard, does it? Is there anything I can get you, Miss Bromwich, before I go?"

"Nothing, thank you. Tell me, isn't today Ward Nine's day for the telephone trolley?"

"Yes, I believe it is."

"Thank you. That's all, Staff. I thought it was."

When Haggerty had gone, closing the door behind her with exaggerated quietness, she rang through to Ward 9 and asked them to connect Rena, if the trolley was free, and if she was well enough.

Rena was well enough. Her voice was bright and confident. "Viv! How are you? I've been enquiring, but you always seemed to be asleep."

"I'm better. Rena, the Haggerty girl has just been to see me."

"She has? I hope you remembered to call her 'Sister' now she's been promoted?"

"No, I didn't, as a matter of fact. Did you know the rest of her news?"

Even if Rena knew she didn't say so. She simply listened. When Vivien stopped talking she said, "Do you mind awfully?"

"That's the idiotic thing! I don't mind a bit. I—I think it's rather amusing, as a matter of fact. Is that crazy?"

"No. It's a natural reaction, I'd say. I can understand it."

"Good. I was beginning to wonder whether I was hysterical."

Rena hesitated, and then she said, "Viv, I didn't tell you what I wanted to. About—Paulson. Do you want to hear it now, or when you see me?"

"I may as well hear it now. It will probably sound just as improbable as what I've just heard. Go on."

"I told you I knew Dr. Catlow, Viv?"

"Yes. I suppose he was—your husband?"

Rena's laugh rang out, crackling in the receiver. "Is *that* what you thought? Oh, no. He wasn't. . . . Damn they want the phone for somebody else. I can't talk an, more, Viv. Come and see me when you can?"

"I will. 'Bye." She put the telephone down, and as she did so she noticed the grotesque little cactus, still standing there in its pot, as ugly as ever, and smiled. And then she looked across at Johnny's yellow chrysanthemums, already beginning to look tired in the centrally-heated atmosphere. The cactus, whether it bloomed or not, would certainly outlast them, she thought.

Winnie brought her a tea-tray, and said, "Fancy, Mr. Cartwright's back. Brought him by air ambulance, so Mr. MacBain was saying."

"Thank you, Winnie. I was just longing for a cup of tea. . . . Is he really? That's good news. I suppose he's warded, though?"

"Oh, yes. But they say he only has the rocking-bed treatment now. That's good, isn't it? We *were* upset when we heard about him—he's such a nice gentleman. There's two new doctors come today too."

Vivien poured her tea and looked up. Winnie, in her better moods, was a mine of gossip. "Oh?"

"Yes, that's right. Two young 'uns. One's the Casualty H.S., and the other's on surgical."

"They haven't replaced *me*, I hope!"

"Oh, no, I shouldn't think so. But with Mr. Dysart going away and everything, they've been a bit shorthanded, I expect. Poor Mr. Clements, he's been run right off his feet this last day or two. Me and Dorothy, we've been fed up with him always being late to his meals, I can tell you."

She felt guilty, then, for wondering why Dick hadn't been in to see her. Instinctively, she glanced at his spiky little gift. Winnie's eyes moved round, following hers. "That's one of them quick-blooming things, isn't it, Miss Bromwich? Queer, aren't they? You ever seen one come out?"

"No, never. Have you?"

153

Winnie nodded enthusiastically. "My auntie had one. The chap she had it from told her it'd only be in flower for about an hour, and she was to wish on it while it was full out."

"And did she?"

"She did. *And* she came up on the pools that week too! Mind you, she set up half the night watching it, in case it came out while she was asleep." She leaned over the plant pot and pursed her lips. "Won't be long before that one comes out, I'd say. Lovely flower they are, too. Red."

"I shall look forward to that, Winnie."

"Yes, well, I've got to go now. Expect Mr. Clements will be late again, and shouting for a fresh pot of tea."

Vivien wanted to say, "Give him my love. Ask him to come and see me." But you couldn't say those things to Winnie. She only smiled instead, as the girl went out.

By the time Home Sister came up, before going off duty, she was up and dressed and standing restlessly at the window, looking across at the empty park. Sister said, "Depressing spectacle, isn't it, at this time of year?"

Vivien nodded. "Yes, very depressing. Not much to see, is there?" And she was seeing Arnold Paulson bending over her in the boat. She shivered, and turned away.

"You're not cold, are you? You shouldn't have got up today."

"No, I'm not cold. And I feel perfectly well, Sister, so don't fuss. I must get back to work soon."

"Not today, Miss Bromwich. I'm sure Dr. Palmer won't hear of it."

"Do you think he'll hear of my visiting Miss Todd? If I promised to go to bed again early?"

Sister frowned thoughtfully. "We-e-ell. . . . It might do Miss Todd good. You won't get chilled, will you, now?"

"I won't. I promise. I'll put my thickest woolly on."

"Well then, you're the doctor, as they say. But do be sensible, Miss Bromwich, won't you?" She walked idly over to tidy the bed-table, and, like Winnie, looked curiously at Dick's cactus. "I wonder whether it'll bloom for you?"

"Why for *me?* Don't they bloom for everyone?"

154

Sister's eyes widened. "Indeed they don't. It's supposed to be very lucky if they do. I suppose that's an old wives' tale, like the way they say they only bloom once in seven years, but it's a fact that they're hard to rear, and they only bloom for a few people. People with green fingers, maybe."

"I don't think I have them."

"Rubbish, Miss Bromwich! All surgeons have green fingers. Look at Mr. Malcolm—he could put onions in and have dahlias come up. He won at his local flower show year after year with his sweet peas too. I wonder what's to happen to that lovely garden of his? A pity to see it go to strangers."

Sister would hear soon enough, Vivien decided. Rena hadn't made any secret of it. "It isn't going to strangers, Sister. Between you and me, it's going to Miss Todd."

"*Really?* Well, isn't that nice? I wonder whether she'll let me have some cuttings from that buddleia of his? I've always wanted to try it."

"I'm sure she will, Sister. But better not say anything yet. Wait till the news gets out."

To judge from Sister's expression, that would not be long, Vivien realised.

Sister White met her at the door of Ward 9. "You're better, then, Miss Bromwich?" She glanced at Vivien's white jacket. "Back on duty already?"

"No, not really. I just feel odd walking round the wards without a jacket, that's all. As though I were just a visitor. I came to see Miss Todd, if that's all right."

"Perfectly all right, Miss Bromwich, if you're sure you're well. Go right in." She opened the linen-room door. "I must finish my report before Nurse Wentworth arrives, if you'll excuse me."

Rena was feeling better, that was plain. She had lipstick on again, and that was a sure sign with any patient. "Showing the flag", the men called it. She smiled up at Vivien. "Lovely. I didn't expect this."

"Sheer curiosity brought me," Vivien confessed. "I wanted to hear the rest of the story." And then, as Rena's face clouded, she added, "That's if you feel like it."

"Of course. Sit down, Viv. It's not pretty, but I want

155

you to know—now. After all that's happened. I told you I felt to blame."

Vivien drew up the chair and sat down. "Go on, then. And you're not to blame in the least, so do forget that aspect of it." She looked out of the window at the lights of the House across the grounds. "You said Dr. Catlow wasn't your husband. That's as far as we got."

Rena lay back and closed her eyes. "He was my husband's friend, Viv. He was older than we were. A good man. We—we sort of turned to him with our woes, at times. He was a pretty nice person. When—when the other girl came along, I went to him for advice."

"What did he say?"

"He said, 'Nothing matters now but the child,' and advised me to go on as though nothing had happened. And I did. God knows I did."

"Rena, don't tell me all this if it upsets you."

"No, I want to. It's all old history. Ted Catlow was a sort of sheet-anchor to me just then. And when—when I got to the end of my tether——" Her voice trailed off.

"You had an affair with him?"

Rena grimaced. "I tried to. But he wouldn't play. I must have put him in some pretty compromising positions, one way and another. Letters . . . and calling at his place at all hours. Oh, I was insane a little, just then."

Vivien understood then: "And Paulson knew all that?"

"Exactly. *And* made capital of it. There hadn't really been anything between Ted and me, beyond a friendly kiss or two. But you could make it sound a lot worse if you wanted to. And Paulson did want to. I—I had to buy him off." She looked up. "That's all, really."

"He's tried that game since he's been here?"

"Oh, no!" Rena laughed. "Once my husband was dead it didn't matter to me any more. And he died soon after Ted Catlow. But I was still knocked sideways when he came here. I didn't know what to do, whether to expose him, or—— But there wasn't a thing that I could pin down, to tell the H.G., was there? He wasn't doing any harm, he wasn't pretending to be anything he wasn't. For all I know he was trying to 'go straight,' as it's called. It wasn't until——" She frowned, and stopped talking.

"I know. I'm glad you told me, Rena. I've been the biggest *fool!* Have you forgiven me for being such an idiot?"

"Of course." Rena touched her hand. "Now forget it all. It's over. The courts will deal with him. And as for her, I suppose he must have had some hold over her too, or she'd never have stuck by him as she did. They were just a couple of orphans, you know, fighting to be somebody."

Vivien stood up. "I'm going now. You've talked enough." She bent to kiss Rena's cheek. "I'll come again tomorrow."

She waited, along the flat, looking out of the window until Sister White went off duty, and then walked back to the main door of Ward 9. It was just possible that Dick might be there. But she could only see Nurse Wentworth and her junior, scanning the written report again at the desk. So as to make quite sure, she walked the length of the ward, and went through on to the outside staircase at the far end, so as not to disturb the patients again.

Somebody was rattling down the iron stairs from the floor above, and she stood back to let him pass. Dick walked straight past her in the darkness and went into the ward. Without thinking twice, she followed him.

Halfway along the dimly-lit row of beds he stopped to reach down a chartboard, and then slipped it back on to its rack. "Vivien," he breathed. "It's been so long, this last day or two." He touched her arm. "Are you quite better?"

She trembled at the warm aliveness of his fingers. "Yes, I'm better. And I've been thinking."

His eyes gleamed in the light from the far table, where Nurse Wentworth still bent over the report book. "Something to tell me?"

"I—I think so."

He took her hand, and led her to the ward door. "The round can wait for a little," he said. "This is more important. And I've something to tell you too."

They both smiled at Nurse Wentworth as she came to meet them, putting on her cuffs. "Ring if you want me, Nurse," Dick told her. "I'll be back later."

He took her down in the lift to the ground floor, and

urged her out along the front hall to the little-used R.S.O.'s office. "It's warm in here," he told her, as he switched on the light. When the door was shut behind them, and he had drawn the heavy green curtains over the casement window, he turned to her with both arms outstretched. "I think you need a little help," he said shakily. "Let me give it to you, Vivien."

He held her very close, quivering with tension, before he let her go again and asked, "What have you decided, Viv? You *have* decided, haven't you?"

She nodded. "Yes, I've decided, Dick. I told you—I love you."

When she saw his face, she knew just how much love he had to give her too. "Thank God!" he murmured. And then his mouth came down to find hers, and she was no longer unsure of anything. It seemed that her whole life had fallen beautifully into place, and that Dick's sure hands had created something permanent out of chaos. She would never cease to be grateful to him, she told herself. She began to return his kisses, urgently wanting to give, instead of taking. It had never been like this with Johnny, she realised. As for Paulson—he didn't exist in the same world with Dick. He simply didn't count.

After a long time he lifted his head. "Now my news," he said quietly. "I hope you'll like it, my love. I'm—I'm taking over Mr. Malcolm's work." There was a dimple in his cheek that she had never seen before. "Are you glad?"

"*Glad?* Oh, Dick! Now we have everything."

He let her go. "Everything except time. Viv, I *must* go and work. Forgive me?"

She stood on tiptoe to kiss his cheek. "I wouldn't forgive you if you didn't, my dear."

When she had watched him float up in the lift towards his rounds, she walked slowly back to her room, wrapped in his love and nearness. The moonlight silvered the park railings, and made magic with the filigree of the over-hanging trees, and she wondered why she had thought the view depressing earlier in the day, when it was so beautiful by night.

As soon as she opened her door she walked into a cloud

of fresh sweet perfume, and snapped on the light quickly. On the bedside table Dick's cactus was almost invisible, dwarfed by the great flower, brilliant blood-red, that had unfolded in her absence, curving up and out from the plain little stem like a huge scented butterfly.

She would have liked to wish, as Winnie had told her she should—but there was nothing left to wish for. She had everything.

information please

**All the Exciting News from
Under the Harlequin Sun**

It costs you nothing to receive our news bulletins and intriguing brochures. From our brand new releases to our money-saving 3-in-1 omnibus and valuable best-selling back titles, our information package is sure to be a hit. Don't miss out on any of the exciting details. Send for your Harlequin INFORMATION PLEASE package today.